Gallant Guard-dach

Cozy Mysteries with a Dash of Dachshund

Alice Kanaka

ISBN: 979-8-9894257-7-8
First printing March 2025
Editor: Linda at Victory Editing
Cover: Bookbrush

Table of Contents

More Books by Alice Kanaka

<u>Samantha Olivares Mysteries</u>

The Cardinal & the Crow
The Cardinal, the Fat Boy, & the Flamingo
The Cardinal & the Hawk
The Cardinal & the Crane

<u>Bumfuzzle and Cattywampus: Unlikely Detectives</u>

Trouble at the Buckeye Festival
Mystery at Rutherford Mansion

<u>Mavis & Hornwhistle</u>

Winter Wonderdach
Gallant Guard-dach

<u>Standalone</u>

Pious Assassin

Chapter 1

Snowbound

Lizzy stared out her front window, unsure how to feel about the four-foot-tall snowdrifts decorating her yard. *Holly made it out of town just in time. I wish I could have gone with her.* Lizzy imagined basking in the Florida sun and sighed, then looked down at her miniature dachshund. "Let's try the back."

Mavis, already dressed in her warm winter coat, barked and pranced impatiently while Holly's tiny kitten, Candy, trailed along, leaping into the air in an attempt to catch Mavis's long wagging tail. They followed Lizzy to the back, where she grabbed Candy as Mavis shot through the French doors.

The covered back porch was traversable, but the snow in the yard was much too deep and icy for the little dog. Leaving the kitten inside, Lizzy scanned the backyard before picking Mavis up and carrying her to the raised gazebo.

The wind blew the snow from the west, creating a barrier on the left and an almost-clear patch on the right. She fell several times as the crusty snow broke under her feet, jarring her teeth and her back. As a potty spot, the gazebo wasn't ideal, but it would do in an emergency. She set Mavis down on the frozen, snow-dusted dirt below the structure.

"I'm sorry. I'll shovel a better spot for you later." Mavis ran back and forth around the space, sniffing carefully. "Hurry up, puppy. I'm freezing."

Mavis finally assumed the position and remained for thirty seconds. Lizzy counted.

"You must have been holding that for a while."

Mavis trotted back to Lizzy and wagged her tail. "Ahrooherer."

"I hear you. It's breakfast time, isn't it."

"Roherer."

Candy was waiting for them, her tiny paws on the glass doors. Once back inside, Lizzy prepared their breakfast and placed the bowls on the floor. Having just recently graduated from formula, Candy went right to work on her food, but Mavis sat and stared at hers, thwacking the floor twice with her tail.

"My apologies, Your Majesty. Where is my head this morning?" Lizzy bent and gave Mavis a little neck-and-shoulder massage. "You good now?"

Mavis was busy eating.

After starting a pot of coffee and sticking an onion bagel in the toaster, Lizzy went into the living room to make a fire. She pondered her predicament and thought it would be more fun to experience her first blizzard with a friend. Between books, she had sunk into the weird phase that always hit when she finished one and hadn't yet begun the next. She felt restless and bored. Holly's absence and the snow only exacerbated the situation.

She shuffled back into the kitchen for her breakfast and found Mavis watching her expectantly.

"Don't even think about it. I just fed you."

<hr>

The streets of Harperstown were quiet under a thick blanket of snow, the only sound emanating from the engine of Jason's Ski-Doo superwide-track snowmobile. Although clothed in multiple layers of winter gear, he shivered. The loud growl of a chainsaw competed with the sound of his engine as he drove down Main Street and pulled up in front of Lizzy's house. A short, stocky man unrecognizable under his snowsuit, cap, and goggles was using the saw to cut a notch at the base of Lizzy's fifty-foot pine tree.

Jason eyed the soaring pine and the space between the two homes, then shut off his snowmobile and slogged through the snow, shouting, "Stop!" and waving his arms.

The man couldn't hear him over the chainsaw, but Jason's movements must have caught his eye. He cut the motor. "What?" he demanded with a scowl.

"You need a permit and tree-removal professionals for that."

"I'm a licensed contractor. I guess I know how to cut down a tree."

"It's not your tree, and it's dangerous. I'll have to give you a fine if you continue."

"Who are you? The tree police?" He revved up the saw and went back to work without waiting for an answer.

Jason didn't waste any time. He trudged up Lizzy's steps and pounded on her door.

When she opened it, he scanned her intelligent brown eyes and her disheveled blonde hair and realized he had missed her. "Grab Mavis and Candy and come with me. Some lunatic next door is cutting down your tree."

Her thin lips formed a small O as she backed away from the door. Handing him Mavis and her doggy coat, Lizzy grabbed hers from the closet and shrugged into it as she left the entrance and called Holly's kitten.

In minutes, they were on the snowmobile, headed away from the house. Lizzy held on to Jason with one arm and Mavis with the other while keeping Candy tucked inside her coat.

She leaned forward. "Brr. Where are we going?"

"Dave's," he hollered over his shoulder. "The diner's closed, but he invited me for lunch. I hope that tree doesn't fall on your house."

"Can he do that? It's in my yard."

"Short of arresting him, I couldn't stop him, but he'll end up in court."

"Who is he? I haven't even met him yet."

"I heard Ethel left her house to her brother."

"Figures," Lizzy muttered into his ear.

Jason had to agree. Ethel Crocker, Lizzy's former neighbor, had been a middle-aged widow with a penchant for peeping through windows and spreading gossip.

———————

Discombobulated to say the least, Lizzy hadn't expected anyone to stop by and certainly hadn't anticipated being whisked away on a snowmobile. Vaguely worried about her neighbor and the tree, she was nevertheless pleased with the change of scenery. "Where is everyone?" she asked. "It's like a ghost town."

"The plows couldn't keep up. Most people are hunkering down at home."

"Have you been going in to work?"

"Yeah, but even the criminals are snowed in. We've been sitting around, watching movies between calls." He pulled up next to several snowmobiles, parked diagonally where the curb might have been, and helped Lizzy dismount.

Mavis barked at the wind and wagged her tail.

The dog was warming up to Dave and only barked twice when he opened the door for them.

A beer stein in one hand and a broad smile that tempered his slightly sinister appearance, he welcomed them heartily. "Come on in out of the cold. I see you brought Mavis."

"And Candy too," Lizzy said, gently extracting the kitten from her coat.

"She's so tiny. Can I hold her?" He extended a wide palm.

"Of course. I'm cat-sitting for Holly."

Dave took the tiny ball of white fluff and held her close. "I have dogs, but I have to admit to a weakness for kittens. She's a cutie."

Mavis, protective of Candy, jumped on Dave's leg and barked.

"Is she good with her?"

"She's adopted her."

Nodding, he put the kitten down next to Mavis. "We'll have to be careful no one steps on her. Come on into the bar and let me get you a drink."

Sergeant Barker was already seated at one of the round tables, next to a voluptuous young woman with long silky blonde hair and straight white teeth.

"Jason. It's been a long time. Why don't you sit here, and we'll catch up?" She patted the chair next to hers.

Jason gazed at her blankly.

"You remember Christine," Dave said. "Christine, this is Lizzy, our newest resident."

"Nice to meet you." Lizzy extended her hand, but Christine ignored it, her perfectly made-up gray eyes focused on Jason.

"You're one of Holly's school friends, right?" Jason nodded at Barker and helped Lizzy with her coat.

"Yes. I'm hoping to see her while I'm here. What's she up to?"

"She's on vacation."

"No, I mean what's she doing? Does she have a job?"

Jason's eyebrows rose. "How long has it been?"

"Ages." She patted the seat next to hers again.

Jason sat between Christine and Barker. Lizzy sat next to Dave on the opposite side of the table. Unlike the fifties-style Formica and black-and-white tiles that decorated the restaurant, the gleaming wood and comfy red chairs in the bar looked slightly more refined. They were designed to create a cozy, relaxed atmosphere where patrons could take their time and order lots of drinks.

Once they were all seated, Pearl, formerly Officer Rice, approached the table to take their orders. She seemed cheerful and friendly, but Lizzy wondered how she felt about waiting on her former boss.

"Coffee all around, Ms. Rice. Then why don't you join us?"

She smiled at Dave and turned toward the bar, her chin-length brown curls bouncing.

"How's she doing?" Jason asked.

"She's great. Your loss is definitely my gain." Dave grinned.

Rice returned with coffee and sandwiches and sat next to him. The soft knit sweater and jeans flattered her petite figure, and Lizzy wondered if she and Dave…

She shook her head. *Mind your own business*, she told herself. *You're getting as bad as the others.* Observing Rice, she couldn't help but notice her change in expression every time she looked at Christine. *She doesn't like Christine. I wonder why.*

"I hear you've been wrangled into helping with Dottie's latest brainchild," Dave said.

Lizzy canted her head, and Rice elbowed him. "I don't think Dottie's asked yet."

Everyone turned toward the door when someone knocked, and Dave rose to unlock it. He returned with Dottie and Steve Peele, both of them unbundling as they approached.

"Hello everyone," Dottie said. Her spiky, pink-tipped hair was slightly flattened by her ski cap, but her husband's beard seemed to have somehow expanded.

"Did you bring me baked goods?" Lizzy asked. "My lack of sweets is seriously damaging my psyche."

Eyes twinkling with mirth, Dottie said, "I'll see what I can do about a special delivery."

"Have you been busy, Doc?" Jason asked.

"Not too bad." Steve used both hands to tamp down his long curly beard. "Most people are staying indoors. There have been a few, like always."

"Dave let the cat out of the bag," Rice said.

"He mentioned you had something you wanted me to help with," Lizzy added.

"I do. Perhaps we can discuss it when I deliver your baked goods." Dottie sat on Lizzy's left and gave her a little side hug.

Eyeing her suspiciously, Lizzy nodded and helped herself to a sandwich.

She was fairly certain she'd be taking on a new project. So far, she hadn't been able to say no to anything in Harperstown.

While keeping one eye on Christine, she listened to everyone discussing the weather and what they'd been up to behind the blanket of snow. Christine leaned in toward Jason, whispering in his ear and running her hand down his sweater sleeve, as if smoothing out imaginary wrinkles.

Jason stiffened and leaned away.

"He's not interested," Dottie whispered.

"What? Oh. It's none of my business anyway."

"It could be if you wanted it to."

Lizzy didn't look at Dottie, but she thought about her words. *Do I want it to be? No. I don't want to go there. Not after last time.*

"Where's Harvey?" she asked Jason.

"He's at home. He doesn't do snowmobiles."

"He and Mavis need to have a playdate."

"I'll have to figure out how to get him over to your house."

"What if we drop Mavis and Candy off and go pick him up? I could hold on to him on the back."

"Can you drive a snowmobile?"

"I've never tried. I can drive a motorcycle."

"Then you drive, and I'll hold Harvey. That'll be easier."

Neither one of them mentioned the very real possibility that Lizzy's house might no longer be habitable. *Cross my fingers it's okay,* she thought.

"Are you ready to go?" Jason asked, rising. Christine pouted.

"Yes. Thanks for your hospitality, Dave. Do we owe you anything?"

"No, today it's on the house. I'm glad of the company."

"It's been great to get out," she agreed, looking around for Mavis. *I should have known.* Lying in front of a roaring fire Lizzy hadn't noticed on previous visits, Candy looked like the coconut center of her dachshund donut.

"Come on, you two," she called, only to be ignored. "Little stinkers," she muttered.

Jason said, "You get your coat on and grab Candy, and I'll get Mavis into hers."

Lizzy was grateful for his help. The two animals liked to run in opposite directions when she tried to corral them at home.

They said goodbye to their friends and left the diner. Lizzy's house was only a block from Dave's, but they traveled slowly on the icy snow. As they approached the intersection, a snowmobile heading in the opposite direction ran the stop sign.

Jason shook his head. "That was your neighbor. It looked like his passenger was holding an overnight bag. Want to take bets?" He stopped at the curb, and they stared at the damage. The fifty-foot pine had fallen on the neighbor's house, crushing the two top floors in the process. "I guess issuing a ticket would be senseless at this point."

"You might be right. Poor guy."

Jason made a noncommittal sound. "I warned him. I told him he needed a permit and to hire professionals. It could have landed on *your* house."

"Was that his wife with him?"

"Probably. Now *her* you can feel sorry for."

"It looks bad. I wonder if they'll rebuild."

"I don't know. When we get a thaw, they'll have water damage too."

Poor people. What would I do if that was my house? Would I try to rebuild? I would have to move out until it got fixed. Where would I live?

"What?" Jason was talking to her.

"Let's get Mavis and Candy inside. I'm going to have to inspect the damage and track him down. I'll shovel a potty spot when I get back."

Chapter 2

Mrs. Fickle's Secret

Jason called Barker and explained the situation. As he waited for his sergeant, he pulled off his ski cap and ran a hand through his curly red hair. The cap, combined with his helmet, made his head sweat, and he knew from experience that his hair would freeze solid. He replaced the cap and walked the perimeter of the house, noting the extensive damage. Not only had the tree crushed the top floors, but the impact had also broken most of the windows, the pressure making the front door unusable.

Barker pulled up on his snowmobile and joined him where he was standing at a distance. "Bad time for that to happen," he said.

Jason nodded. "We need to make sure the gas is turned off and the fire's out, but I'm not sure if it's safe to go inside. It looks like the whole house might collapse."

"Why don't we call Byron? He might have some advice. And we can check through the windows for the fireplace. Where are the owners?"

"I don't know, but if I had to take a guess, I'd say they're at the hotel. They haven't been here long enough to make friends. Call the chief, and I'll start looking for the fireplace."

Jason strode back toward the house as Barker dialed, occasionally potholing as he tried to avoid the deep drifts. He listened intently for creaking wood or breaking glass. *I'll start with the front windows.* All the 1900s Queen Ann–style homes along Main Street varied in their layout, so he wasn't surprised when the fireplace was located in a different room than the one in Lizzy's.

He walked the perimeter again, away from the tree, checking in windows as he went.

When Barker caught up with him, he said, "I've found one in here, and it's not lit, but I can't be sure it's the only one. What did Byron have to say?"

"He's on his way. He said not to go inside until he checks for a gas leak."

"Let's keep looking then."

"What was going on with Christine?"

"I have no idea. I don't even really remember her."

"She seemed like she was marking her territory." Barker shrugged. "Personally, I prefer Lizzy."

Jason concentrated on keeping his face blank, but he could feel his shoulders stiffen. *Of course he likes Lizzy. Who wouldn't?*

"Not for me," Barker said. "For you. I like her. She's funny and smart."

Jason's shoulders relaxed, and he changed the subject as if it didn't matter. "I've found the fire. How're we going to put it out?" He pointed through one of the back windows. "There's a cat in there."

"Try the door."

Jason turned the knob and found it locked. "Now what?"

"I can open it." Lizzy's voice startled him. "But you have to close your eyes."

"Where did you come from? And why do I have to close my eyes?"

"Because if you see how I open the door, you might take away my toys."

Barker chuckled when Jason rolled his eyes. "Come on, Cap, let's play along. We need to rescue the kitty."

Sighing, Jason followed Barker's lead and turned his back to the door. He heard the jangle of keys and the sound of the door being unlocked, then turned back in time to see Lizzy putting her hand in her coat pocket.

"Ta-da," she sang.

"I'm not sure what to do with you."

"You must admit I'm handy. I came over to tell you about the cat. I've seen her outside." Lizzy tried and failed to pick the cat up, then chased her when she ran inside.

"No. Lizzy, stop. The house isn't safe." Jason heard her say something as she passed into the kitchen but couldn't make out her words. "Should I go in after her?" he asked Barker.

"Byron's here. Let's ask him."

"Ask me what?" Crunching toward them, a yellow handheld device in one gloved hand, the fire chief ran the other over his substantial frozen mustache.

"Lizzy ran into the house to save the cat. Should I go in after her?"

"Stay here. I have to go inside to use the monitor anyway. I'll warn her. I wish I had the truck. That fire needs to be put out as well. Maybe they have a bucket handy. We need to hurry."

The chief went inside, and the cat, a large orange-and-white tabby, ran out the door, followed by Lizzy.

"Close the door," she said, the deep snow thwarting her attempt to chase the cat. "At least she's out of the house. Maybe I should go back in and get her food."

"No!" Jason and Barker said in unison.

"What's going on?"

"The house isn't safe. Byron's checking for gas leaks, but we need to stay out of there," Jason said. "I'll ask the homeowners their cat's name and what she eats. Holly will have some." His sister carried a little of everything in the pet shop attached to her clinic. He was fairly sure it didn't make a profit, but she always had supplies on hand. *She's the best kind of vet. She always puts her patients first.*

"I wish she was here. She'd know what to do. That cat might freeze to death."

"Where is she now?"

"Up there." Lizzy pointed to a nearby tree.

He and Barker looked up at the pine.

"Keep an eye on her. I'll see what Byron thinks. He has cats."

The fire chief was on his way out of the house and stopped to speak to Jason. "No gas leaks. I put the fire out, but you should post signs warning everyone to stay away."

"Do you have any idea how to capture a frightened cat?"

"That's such a huge question. It depends on the cat and the situation."

"The cat who lives here is up in that tree."

"Do they have a ladder?"

"Probably."

"I have one," Lizzy said. "It's on the back porch."

"I'll go get it." They watched Barker crunch through the snow with long strides.

A few minutes later, he reappeared with an extension ladder balanced on one shoulder like Atlas. "Where do we want this?"

Byron showed him where to put the ladder. "You two spot me. I'll go up." The cat, frightened and freezing, still resisted when Byron scooped her up and zipped her into his warm coat. "I'll have some scars from this one," he said as he reached the bottom. "Lizzy, can we take her to your house?"

"Yes, but I don't know much about cats. Holly's kitten is the first one I've ever taken care of."

"Put her in a small room, away from the other pets, until she settles down. You'll need to get them used to each other little by little."

"A spare bedroom? I wish I had some of her things. Can't I go inside and get her bed?"

Byron looked over his shoulder at the house, then shook his head.

"Let's just get her to your place," Jason said. "I'll take you over to Holly's to get a few things. We still have work to do."

Lizzy sat on the bed in one of the spare bedrooms and watched her new houseguest. She decided to call the cat Marmalade since she didn't know her name and talked to her as she prepared a sandbox and poured some food into a bowl. She placed the new bed next to the cat and picked up a brush.

"Do you like to be brushed?" She held it up for Marmalade to see.

Locked in a staring contest for a moment, Lizzy thought the cat wasn't interested, but then with a soft meow, Marmalade launched herself onto the bed and rubbed her cheek against the stiff bristles.

Lizzy gently brushed the cat, torn between her comfort and the pitiful whining and scratching in the hall. "I know, Mavis. I'll be out in a minute."

Her phone vibrated, and she paused to see who was calling. Sage Fickle. She must be back. Marmalade pushed her cheek against the brush again, knocking the phone out of Lizzy's hand.

"So impatient. All of you." Lizzy resumed brushing with one hand as she bent to retrieve the phone.

"Hello, Mrs. Fickle," she answered. "Are you home?"

"I am. Can you meet me in the basement? It's time I show you the passage and tell you the rest of the story."

Remembering Mrs. Fickle's mysterious visit in December and her hints about a secret tunnel and an escape route, Lizzy said, "Sure. Do you know anything about cats?"

Mrs. Fickle chuckled. "At my age, I know a little bit about everything. Take the key I gave you down to the basement. Go past the water heater and look for the wall sconce. Twist it to the left, and the pantry shelves will move aside, giving you access to the door."

"Okay. See you in a few." Disconnecting, Lizzy gave Marmalade a final brush and said, "I'll be back soon." Then she carefully let herself out of the room, holding Mavis back with a foot. "Come on, troublemaker. We're going on a little adventure."

The key Mrs. Fickle had given her was in a small box on one of her bookshelves, so she retrieved it and picked Candy up before heading downstairs. Remembering her first visit to the basement, she shivered involuntarily. An intruder had flipped the breakers, leaving her without light, and she had followed Jason down into the dark unknown when he arrived to investigate. Now, with illumination, an alarm system, and familiarity, it was just another room—mostly.

Lizzy followed Sage Fickle's instructions and unlocked the door to find her smiling neighbor waiting on the other side. She hadn't seen her for over a month, not since Christmas. "You're looking great, Mrs. Fickle. Much more relaxed."

"Thank you, dear." Mrs. Fickle bent to pet Mavis, her long, gray braid falling over her shoulder. "Hello, sweet puppy." She smiled when Lizzy helped her straighten, showing her crooked front tooth. "I must admit I'm feeling much better. Why don't we walk to the other end so you can see the entrance on my side?"

Strolling along the passage, Mrs. Fickle said, "Dottie invited me to meet with the two of you in about an hour, so I thought this would be a good opportunity to talk to you." She stopped and unlocked the door to her basement. "The entrance on this side is exactly the same as the one on your end; the sconce activates the mechanism that moves the shelves."

"Does your husband know about this?"

"No…" Mrs. Fickle relocked the door and began leading the way back toward Lizzy's house. "I can see I'll have to explain some things. Do you happen to have some tea? I have a little chill."

"Yes. Come on into the kitchen, and when we're done, I'll introduce you to my temporary houseguest."

Mrs. Fickle glanced at her.

"The neighbor's cat. Did you hear about the tree?"

"Yes. Even holed up in a blizzard, gossip still manages to spread like wildfire."

"Amazing," Lizzy mumbled.

Mavis, still trotting along with the two unlikely friends, barked and wagged her tail when they entered the kitchen. Lizzy pulled Candy out of her jacket and handed her to Mrs. Fickle before filling a stove-top kettle with water and retrieving a box of tea bags.

"Is this your houseguest?" She sat at the table.

"Yes and no. Candy is Holly's kitten. I'm watching her while Holly's out of town."

"She's precious." Holding Candy up to look at her tiny face and whispering endearments, Mrs. Fickle's eyes got misty. "It's been a long time since I've held a kitten."

Mavis whined.

"Is this your friend?"

"Ahrooer."

"Take good care of her." Mrs. Fickle put the kitten next to Mavis, who gave her a lick and wagged her tail.

Lizzy placed two cups of tea on the table, then sat down across from Mrs. Fickle. "Let's hear the story. I can hardly contain my curiosity."

"Where to begin? Let's see. You know about Percy and the business with my cousin, right?"

Lizzy nodded. "Sort of."

"My family hasn't always been on the right side of the law, especially the older generations. My father wanted me out of it, so he agreed to my marriage to an outsider, but he had certain rules. One of his rules was that I always have my own money and that I have a safe house that no one knows about, even him."

Lizzy's eyebrows rose. "If you tell me, aren't you breaking the rules?"

"Yes, but he passed many years ago, and if anything happens to me, the house and my savings will be lost." She paused and gazed at Lizzy. "Also, if I need to use the house for some reason, I'd like someone to know where I am, someone who won't divulge my whereabouts to the wrong people."

"That sounds rather sinister. Are you expecting trouble?"

"I don't know any details about your past, but I think you might understand. You've thought about what might happen if certain people find out where you are."

"Are you hiding out from your family?"

"No, they know where I am. They keep an eye on me. I felt safe when Percy and I were well out of it, but then he had to get involved. I asked him not to. Now he's in jail, and the family is rethinking what they know about me."

Puzzled, Lizzy tried to figure out what Mrs. Fickle might be hiding. She struggled to focus because her writer's brain was rapidly conjuring an intriguing plot. She needed to write it down before she forgot, but she knew Mrs. Fickle was counting on her. "Could I... Just a second, okay? I need to write down an idea, and then I'll be able to focus. Just... please? I'm sorry." She stood and strode to her desk to grab a pen and a pad of paper.

A few minutes later, she returned to the table and resumed her seat. "I'm really sorry. I wouldn't have been able to hold a normal conversation until I wrote it down."

Mrs. Fickle's lips turned up slightly. "It's a blessing and a curse, isn't it?"

Lizzy nodded.

"I'm glad that my story was able to inspire you in some way."

"I'm sure it wasn't your actual story, because I still don't understand. What does your family think you might be hiding?"

"We'll leave that for now. Let's talk about you. I've heard the rumors, but why did you really come to Harperstown?"

With a deep sigh, Lizzy said, "I don't know how it happened. I had a quiet life. I lived with my fiancé, spent most of my time writing, and went out occasionally with a small group of friends I've known since I was in high school. I thought everything was fine until my fiancé dumped me, calling me a boring mooch. I needed support, but my friends didn't want to hear about it, so I felt very alone.

"Then my newest book went viral and got signed for a movie deal, and I can't even explain what happened. My life turned upside down. I suddenly had lots of money, but I couldn't leave my house. The paparazzi were everywhere. They climbed my back fence and peeped in my windows. One even pretended to deliver a package and hid around the corner waiting for me to open the door. If I went to the grocery store, supposed fans would surround me, demanding autographs and sometimes getting violent.

"I ended up in the hospital twice." She shook her head. "My ex and the friends who didn't have time for me when I needed them sold stories and photos to the press. I didn't know what to do, so I called my attorney and asked for help."

"My family could have helped you," Mrs. Fickle said wryly. "Like making a deal with the devil though."

"I did need to keep my real identity for business purposes."

"True. So, if they find out you're living here, they'll come in droves. Is that it?"

"More or less."

"There's an unregistered vehicle in my garage that I don't drive. The key is on a hook in the passage. Dottie will be here soon, but this envelope contains the GPS coordinates to the house. Put it somewhere safe. I'll take you there when we have a thaw and show you the security system. It's complicated."

"Why me? You hardly know me."

Mrs. Fickle patted her hand. "I know people." She smiled. "And my escape route might come in handy for you too. We'll talk details later."

Mavis began barking, signaling Dottie's arrival a second before the bell rang.

Chapter 3

Operation Valentine

Dottie stood on the porch, her cheeks almost as pink as her lipstick. Her youthful face and demeanor were at odds with her pink-tipped white hair, making it difficult for Lizzy to guess her age. *In her late forties, perhaps.* She was friends with Holly and Holly's mother.

"May I come in?" Dottie's blue eyes sparkled with mirth.

"Yes, sorry."

Mavis barked happily and wagged her tail.

"Hello, Mavis. Sage. Have you told Lizzy about our project?"

"No, I'll leave that to you."

"Would you like some tea?" Lizzy asked as she waited for Dottie to scratch Mavis' ears and remove her coat.

"Have you learned how to make a proper cup?"

"She has not."

"We'll have to work on that. Do you have any coffee? I brought goodies."

"I always have coffee on. More tea, Mrs. Fickle?"

"Yes, please. What did you bring, Dottie?"

"Cranberry-orange scones, chocolate croissants, and onion bagels."

"All my favorites!" Lizzy clapped her hands with glee.

"Hopefully they'll tide you over until the thaw."

"You've made me a very happy camper. How much do I owe you?"

"Don't worry about that. Baking's helping me get through this lull. My kitchen is overflowing."

"Just like Holly."

"You miss her, don't you."

"So much."

"Well, let's have a little snack, and I'll tell you about our project. We'll want Holly's help too when she gets back."

As they moved into the kitchen, Dottie asked, "What's wrong with Mavis?"

"She's letting me know it's dinner time. I'll take care of that while you get settled." Lizzy turned on the burner under the kettle and poured Dottie a cup of coffee, then retrieved Mavis' bowl while calling to Candy.

The kitten yawned widely as she entered the room, then pounced on Mavis' tail before climbing Lizzy's leg with her sharp little claws.

"Owww." Lizzy dropped the bowl and grabbed Candy, placing her on her shoulder. "You're such a little devil." She held on to the kitty as she bent to pick up the bowl and proceeded to prepare their meal, making sure to give Mavis her doggy massage and separating their bowls to give Candy a head start. Mavis, the canine vacuum, took a proprietary interest in any food within her reach.

Finally seated with her guests, Lizzy picked up a scone and closed her eyes as she breathed in the sweet scents of orange and cranberry. "You're a genius," she told Dottie and took her first bite.

"Clever tactic," Sage mumbled.

Lizzy took another bite and canted her head. "Tactic?"

"Don't mind her." Dottie smiled. "Do you want to hear about Operation Valentine?"

Sage smirked.

"I'll bite. No pun intended. Let's hear it."

"We've all been cooped up, and we need an event. Also, several houses around here are vacant. So we thought it would be fun and good publicity for the neighborhood if we held a kind of Valentine's-themed mystery maze. Sage volunteered her house for the event, and since you're a writer, we thought you could come up with a scenario. What do you think?"

Staring at her, Lizzy asked, "Who's we?"

"The decorations committee. Will you help us?"

"I've never done anything like that. What exactly would I have to do?"

"We don't really know either. That's why we need your help. We need some kind of interesting activity that can accommodate lots of people with minimal staff. We'll have snacks in the kitchen and a table with prizes for everyone who solves the mystery. We can use the whole house and print out clues. Here's a little map Sage drew." Dottie handed Lizzy a sheet of paper and glanced down at Mavis. "How can you eat with her staring at you like that? Can I give her a piece of my scone?"

Lizzy passed a package of Beggin' Strips to Dottie. "Please don't. You can give her a treat if you like, but sugar's bad for her." She studied the map. "You have secret passages?"

"Isn't it fun? That's one of the reasons we bought the house," Mrs. Fickle said. "They aren't long passages, but there's a secret room and a passage between the library and the master bedroom."

"Whatever the game is, we have to make it easy so guests can move through the house in a short amount of time," Dottie said. "We don't want a line around the block. We could make a more expensive version in the evening, a sort of mystery dinner or something, but this one shouldn't take anyone longer than an hour."

Lizzy stared into space, her mind whirling with possibilities. "Is there a historical mystery or legend we could base it on? Some way to tie in local interest for people from out of town?"

Mrs. Fickle grinned. "There are all kinds of stories about my house and the reason for the secret passages. I'm sure you can use one of them to make a good mystery."

"I'll have to do some research and give it some thought."

"So you'll help?" Dottie asked.

Gazing at her, Lizzy said, "When have I ever been able to say no to you?"

Dottie's eyes twinkled.

"Lizzy rescued the cat next door. Let's go see how she's doing," Mrs. Fickle said.

"Rescued?"

"Didn't you notice the tree?"

Looking perplexed, Dottie shook her head. "I was concentrating on my feet. What happened?"

Lizzy explained on their way upstairs. Running ahead, Mavis stood outside the closed bedroom door and whined. "You stay out here, puppy. We need to give Marmalade some space." That didn't work, of course, so she picked Mavis up and held her until Dottie and Mrs. Fickle were inside. "We'll be right back."

The three women stood in a half circle and observed Marmalade, who was lounging on Lizzy's pillow. Mrs. Fickle was the first to speak. "Just like a cat. She found the most comfortable spot in the room."

Marmalade licked a paw.

"It looks like you've taken care of everything. Food, litter box, bed, toys. She doesn't look stressed or anything," Dottie said.

"I'll be happier when she doesn't have to be shut up by herself. How long do I have to keep her in here?"

"You could try opening the door and seeing how she reacts to Mavis. Since Mavis is smaller than she is, and Candy's a baby, she may not mind them at all. It's hard to say."

"Okay. Here goes." Lizzy opened the door, and Mavis charged in. She looked around expectantly, then ran to the cat bowl and inhaled Marmalade's remaining food.

Marmalade watched from the end of the bed, then gracefully dropped to the floor. Tail wagging, Mavis attempted to give her a sniff when a paw shot out and batted her head. *Whap, whap, whap,* three times in rapid succession.

Backing up slightly, Mavis stared at the aggressive intruder momentarily before turning and leaving the room.

"Well, I guess that sort of solves that problem unless Marmalade decides to take over." Dottie chuckled.

"Take over?"

"You know. The dog bed, the spot in front of the fireplace, Mavis' personal space. I have to get going, but I'll make sure Marmalade's owner knows where she is. Can I bring her by later if she wants to see her?"

"Sure. Do you know her?"

"No, but Steve always seems to know what's going on. I'll get ahold of her."

"Thanks, Dottie. For the baked goods too."

"You're very welcome. I'll see you soon."

Mrs. Fickle waited until Dottie left, then said, "I should go too, but I'll take the tunnel. Let me know when you have an idea, and we can start planning how to set things up."

Lizzy walked with her to the passage door and watched the shelves slide back into place as the door closed behind her.

Chapter 4

Cat Mama

Sitting before the fire with her phone and a notebook, Lizzy was shocked when she glanced at Mavis' bed and saw a giant orange-and-white mound of fur. Mavis was lying a few feet away with her head on her paws.

"This just won't do, will it?" Lizzy stood and went upstairs, returning with Marmalade's bed. Placing the beds equidistant from the fire, Lizzy moved Marmalade to her own bed and helped Mavis and Candy get settled in the other. Then she decided she needed more coffee. When she returned with her cup, Marmalade was back in Mavis' bed and Mavis was in the other. "Whatever works, I guess."

In addition to writing, Lizzy was skilled at research. She jotted down a list of potential scenarios and began looking up facts about Harperstown and the Fickles' house. The glut of information made her head spin. *I need to keep it simple. It's not a book. Although it really could be. Maybe I need to branch out.*

She was pondering the possibility of writing a historical mystery when the barking erupted. Mavis hopped out of the cat bed, jostling Candy in the process, and ran toward the front door as a firm knock sounded. Lizzy shook her head and followed, still unsure whether Mavis had ESP or supersonic hearing.

Pearl Rice was standing on the stoop with a stranger.

"Sorry to bother you," she began. "This is Madeline Prichard, your neighbor. She's been worrying about her cat, and Jason said she was here."

"Nice to meet you." Lizzy stuck out her hand. Madeline was hatless, with straight black hair cut into an asymmetrical bob.

Judging from the fine lines on her face, Lizzy guessed her to be in her forties. "Come on in. She's over by the fire."

She barely touched Lizzy's outstretched hand and spoke in little more than a whisper. "Thank you so much for looking after her. Nap wouldn't let me take her, and I've been so worried." Hurriedly removing her boots, she followed Lizzy into the living room and dropped to her knees by her cat, who opened one eye. "Hello, princess," she crooned. "How's my pretty baby?"

"Is that her name? I've been calling her Marmalade." Lizzy smiled.

"Her name is Cleopatra, Cleo for short. She hates my husband and just tolerates me, but I love her."

"Should I get her things together?"

Not meeting Lizzy's eyes, her gaze shifting from the cat to the window, then to the staircase, Madeline whispered, "Could you keep her for a little while? The hotel doesn't allow pets."

"I guess so. I don't know much about cats, but she seems pretty self-sufficient. I got her some food and a sandbox."

"Thank you so much." Madeline's lip quivered and her face crumpled. "Can I visit her?"

"Of course. Whenever you like." She looked at Rice. "Why don't we go make some tea while Madeline hangs out with Cleo?"

Rice nodded, her brown curls bouncing as she followed Lizzy toward the kitchen. She stopped in the entrance and watched while Lizzy filled the kettle and retrieved a box of tea bags. "The last time I was here Mrs. Crocker was lying on your floor, and I thought you had killed her."

Lizzy nodded. "We don't know each other very well, but I'm sorry you lost your job. Are you doing okay?"

"Yes and no. Becoming a police officer was all I ever dreamed of. Now I don't know what to do. I can't spend the rest of my life working at Dave's. I'll have to train for another career."

"Any ideas so far?"

"No. Not a thing."

"What if you did something related? Like a private investigator or a bounty hunter? A paramedic?"

Staring at her, Rice frowned momentarily. "Yeah. Maybe."

No longer kneeling with Cleo by the fire, Madeline was wandering around the open-plan downstairs and examining the living space when Lizzy and Rice returned with the tea. Mavis followed, wagging her tail. Madeline straightened abruptly from an open drawer when they emerged from the kitchen, her eyebrows pinched together. "I'm sorry. I was just curious about your house. It's so different from ours."

Lizzy was taken aback by Madeline's behavior. She wasn't just wandering around; she had been searching through her personal papers. "Are you looking for anything in particular?"

"N-no," she stammered. "Nap said you're a writer." She lowered her head. "Are you able to make a living at that?"

"I do okay," Lizzy said modestly. "Would you like your tea now?"

"No, thank you. I think I should get back to the hotel. He'll be waiting."

One glance told Lizzy that Rice was back in police mode. "Is that even your cat?" Rice demanded.

"Of course. She was in the house when the police rescued her."

"We gave you time to spend with her, and you were snooping instead. Why?"

Madeline's hands trembled as she pulled her sweater around her thin frame and took a step back. "I'm just nosy. I'm sorry."

"I don't buy that. It's your husband, right? What's he want to know?"

Eyes wide, she shook her head vehemently. "Please don't tell him."

"Answer the question."

"He wanted to know if she has money. I don't know why. I swear."

"You ready to go?" Rice asked.

Madeline nodded. "What should I tell him?"

"You can tell him the truth," Lizzy said. "I spent my inheritance on this house, and I don't have a dime. I don't even have a car. He's lucky that tree didn't land on my house because we'd be going to court." *If he thinks he's going to get me to pay for the damage he caused when he cut down my tree, he's delusional. I should call Kirk just in case. He'll know what to do.*

"Thank you," Madeline whispered.

Rice walked her stiffly to the front door, turning to shake Lizzy's hand. "Sorry about all this."

Lizzy smiled wanly and pulled Rice aside. "Could you let her know that I'd rather she didn't come back until she's ready to take Cleo home? I told her she could come whenever she wants, but…"

"I get it. I'll let her know. Thanks for the career advice, by the way. I appreciate it."

"Anytime." Lizzy's smile was genuine that time.

⁕

As soon as her guests left, Lizzy sat on the sofa and called to the cat. "Marmalade," she said, rather than Cleo, and was rewarded with a lifted head. "You don't like that lady, do you. Why is that?"

Marmalade stood and gave an elaborate stretch before approaching Lizzy with her tail held high like a question mark. Lizzy held out her hand, and the cat rubbed her cheek against it and purred. *So strange. Why would she ignore her owner? I wish Holly was here. She would know.* Then, remembering she wanted to call her lawyer, she picked up her phone and dialed.

"Lizzy!" he greeted her when he answered.

"I know it's been a long time. How's it going?"

"Great. I'm out by the pool."

"Stop rubbing it in. I've been snowed in for days."

Laughing, he said, "I know. I keep an eye on the weather app."

Lizzy shook her head, even though she knew he couldn't see her. Kirk was much more than just her lawyer. He had helped her escape her old life and was a loyal friend. "Something happened here, and I wanted to ask your advice."

"What happened?" he asked, suddenly serious.

Lizzy told him about her neighbor and the tree, then explained about the cat and Madeline's strange behavior. "I'm not sure what it all means, but it occurred to me that he might try to blame his accident on me somehow. Is there anything I can do to protect myself?"

"Other than the fact that it was your tree, he doesn't have a leg to stand on. And he cut it down without your permission and was warned not to by local law enforcement. Unless he's planning to fake an injury on your property or something, I don't see how you are involved at all."

"Thanks. That eases my mind a little. You should visit when it gets warmer. I miss you."

"I might just take you up on that. I'm definitely curious after hearing about your rocky start and your Christmas epiphany. You're not regretting your move?"

"No, except this weather takes some getting used to. Luckily, the house is warm, and Holly helped me get the right clothing. I can't even describe what seven below with a wind chill factor of minus forty feels like. I ran outside with wet hair to take the garbage out one morning and it turned into icicles. I was only outside for a minute."

"What? That's crazy. At least put on a hat."

"I learned my lesson. Trust me."

"How's your little guard dog?"

Lizzy glanced at Mavis lying in Marmalade's bed in front of the fire. "She's being suspiciously quiet today. I'm sure she's coming up with some nefarious plan to get extra food or something."

One of Mavis' ears rose like an antenna.

"Speaking of food, I have to dress for a business dinner. I'll call you soon, okay?"

"All right. Thank you. Have a nice dinner."

"I will. We're going to Stockyards."

"Mmm. I might be a little jealous. You go get ready. I'll talk to you soon." Lizzy's stomach grumbled as she disconnected. She strode into the kitchen to see if she had anything tempting in the freezer.

"Arooherer."

"You ate already."

Pulling out a Tupperware container of mystery food, she stuck it in the microwave on defrost. Mavis began whining and moaning like she hadn't been fed in a week, and Candy initiated her ascent up Lizzy's pant leg. "Okay, okay. Everybody take it easy. I have to eat too."

Chapter 5

Rescue Team

Mayhem. Lizzy woke to Mavis barking. Candy pounced on the covers, and Marmalade was howling from the guest room. "Stoppp." Lizzy flung her covers off and got dressed before releasing Marmalade and dressing Mavis to go outside. She could hear the pounding music before she opened the door, but she wasn't prepared for the blast of noise that hit her when she went outside. Mavis' barking increased in volume as she stood at the edge of the shoveled area, focused on the Prichards' house.

Not seeing any movement next door, Lizzy carefully made her way through the crusty snow to the radio and turned it off. Initially, she didn't hear anything other than Mavis' incessant barking, but then a faint cry for help sounded in the distance.

"Hello?" she called. "Where are you?"

"In here. I fell through the roof."

"I'll call for help. How long ago did you fall?"

"I don't know." The voice sounded fainter.

"Just hold on." She ran for her house. "Quiet, Mavis. Do your job."

Mavis didn't listen of course. She ran behind Lizzy to the door, then stood barking and wagging her tail as Lizzy grabbed her phone to call Jason and led her back outside.

"What's all that racket?" Jason asked when he answered.

"Mavis. There's been an accident. Someone—Mr. Prichard, I think—fell through the roof of his house. I don't know what kind of injuries he has, but he needs help. He's probably freezing too."

"I'll rally the troops. You stay out of that house."

"I will. Hurry, please."

Unsure of how she could help, Lizzy took Mavis back inside and fed her and the cats, but for once her mind wasn't on her task. Her wildly creative brain was picturing Mr. Prichard lying broken and freezing on a bed of sharp wood. Then she pictured rats scurrying around, trying to bite his fingers. She shivered and ran back outside.

Climbing the ladder that was leaning precariously against the side of the house, she felt the heavy tree shift and suddenly wondered if she might be making it worse. "Mr. Prichard, I've called for help. Can you move? I can try to drop a blanket through the hole if you can reach it."

"No. I won't be able to. Thanks for calling though."

The ladder wobbled when Lizzy turned toward the sound of Jason's snowmobile. She held on to the roof and cringed at the look on his face.

He was next to the ladder before she could move. "Climb down. I've got you," he said, grabbing the base and holding it steady.

Jason called Barker and the fire chief, explaining the situation and soliciting advice. The first to arrive, his heart plummeted when he saw the ladder sway. He was off his snowmobile in seconds, taking long strides across the brittle snow. When Lizzy's feet reached solid ground, he placed his hands on her shoulders and looked into her eyes. "What on earth possessed you to climb that ladder? We don't need two accidents to deal with."

"I just... I thought he might freeze. I wanted to drop him a blanket or something, but he said he can't move."

"You have a good heart but try to have some common sense. The whole roof could cave in." Jason saw her face crumple and knew he sounded too gruff. "Come on. It's okay. You just scared me. The others will be here in a minute. Why don't you put on some coffee to keep them warm?"

Lizzy nodded and turned toward her house.

The fire chief pulled up next, cursing under his breath when the snow broke under his boots. "Where is he?"

"Lizzy said he fell through the roof. She was up on the ladder when I got here."

Byron frowned and ran his gloved hand over his mustache. "I guess I'll need to go up. Spot me." He adjusted the ladder and climbed nimbly to the top. Jason watched him lean over and peer through the hole. "I'm Byron Warner, the fire chief. The roads are impassable, and we can't get the fire truck through. I need to ask you some questions so I can figure out how to get you out of there."

"Okay."

"You're currently on the third floor, right? I can't see you from here."

"Third floor, yes. Part of the tree landed on me."

"Does the floor under you feel solid?"

"I don't know. It's creaking."

"Can you assess your injuries? Does anything feel broken? Are you bleeding? Did you hit your head?"

"I might have broken my arm. Other than that, I'm not sure. The tree is pinning me down."

"Can you wiggle your fingers and toes?"

After a pause, Prichard said, "Yes."

"Okay. Give me a minute. I'll be right back."

Byron climbed down and consulted with Jason and Barker. "We're going to need some more help. In order to get him out without further injuries, we'll need some volunteers to go through the house with a foldable stretcher and additional folks outside to hoist the tree. We haven't assessed the interior damage, so we'll need to take precautions. Jason, call Doc Steve and request an airlift. Barker, call Foster and tell him we need help lifting the tree. I'll call for volunteers. I'm guessing we'll need at least eight strong bodies to get him out."

Jason observed Byron and Barker as he dialed Steve Peele. Byron, although a decade older, possessed boundless energy that never failed to spur everyone around him to action.

When Steve answered, Jason explained the situation. "Byron said to call for an airlift. The victim will need medical treatment."

"I'll be there in a few."

Thanking him, Jason disconnected and listened to the end of Barker's conversation.

"Thanks, Bart. We'll see you soon." Barker slid his phone into his coat pocket. "He'll be here within half an hour."

"Does he have some kind of mobile equipment he can use to move the tree?"

"He understands the situation. He said he'll get some buddies to help."

Jason nodded. "Now we wait." He looked up to catch Lizzy watching miserably through her front window. He could see Mavis' head bobbing up and down as she jumped up to see what Lizzy was looking at. *Neither one of them can stand being left out.* He smiled and gave Lizzy a wave before heading back.

Lizzy wasn't alone for long. Mrs. Fickle showed up first, through the basement passage. "I just wanted to warn you dear. You'll be having company soon. Would you like me to make tea?"

Mavis began to bark.

"Aren't you going to get that?" Mrs. Fickle asked.

"She's been barking all morning."

The doorbell rang, and Lizzy sighed. She opened the door for Dottie and saw Rice head up the walkway with Madeline Prichard. Holding the door ajar, she waited, unsurprised to see three more women from the decorations committee disembarking from newly arriving snowmobiles. Holly's old friend Christine arrived with Dave, who headed next door.

Stacy and Coral were the last to enter and were removing their boots when raised voices erupted from the kitchen.

"Uh-oh," Stacy said. "Who's in there?"

The sound of an upended chair and breaking glass joined high-pitched screaming and Mavis' frantic barking. Lizzy sprinted toward the commotion and gently pushed her way through the wall of bodies. Rice, who had professional training, was restraining Christine while Dottie attempted to drag Madeline away from her.

"What's going on?" Lizzy asked loudly.

Christine and Madeline both began speaking at once.

"I'd like you both to leave."

"That's not fair," Christine whined. "She attacked me."

"It's my husband next door. You don't have any business being here," Madeline yelled.

"Both of you. Out."

"Come on," Rice said. "You heard the lady."

"Let go of me." Christine struggled out of Rice's grip and took a swing at Madeline as she walked by.

Madeline stuck out her foot and laughed smugly as Christine tripped and hit the floor. "Stay away from my husband."

Christine got up slowly, pushed her hair out of her face, then lunged, but Rice stood between her and her opponent. "You'd better hope I don't see you alone," she growled. "You won't be laughing if I do."

Rice escorted Christine outside, then returned and approached Lizzy. "If we send them both outside, they'll just get into it again. Can we have Madeline wait in the living area or something?"

"I see your point, but I don't trust her. What were they fighting about?"

"She thinks Christine was having an affair with her husband."

A knock at the door heralded Jason's arrival. "We've called for a helicopter to take Mr. Prichard to the hospital and thought his wife might like to go as well. Is she here?"

"Yes. She was just leaving. Will he be okay?"

"Doc Steve says he was lucky, but he has a lot of superficial wounds and needs a more comprehensive checkup."

"Why don't you come over for supper and you can tell me about the rescue?"

"Best offer I've had all day." He grinned. "Are you ready to go, Mrs. Prichard?"

"Yes, thank you." Madeline joined Jason on the front porch without a glance at Lizzy or Rice.

Chapter 6

Decorations Committee

The kitchen, when Lizzy returned, was much quieter. Each guest held a mug and a paper plate, six seated on the kitchen chairs and the others standing around. On closer inspection, Lizzy spied three bakery boxes filled with Dottie's creations. *Yes! Coffee and pastries. Just what the doctor ordered.* Her stomach grumbled, and she realized she hadn't eaten breakfast.

Mrs. Fickle handed her a cup of coffee and a plate. "You need some sustenance after the morning you've had."

Piling mini quiches and a cranberry-orange scone on the small plate, Lizzy looked around, trying to determine how she would manage. She placed her cup on the edge of the counter and took a bite of quiche. "Delicious," she mumbled. Her stomach growled again.

Mavis stood at her feet, staring intently, and Lizzy blushed when she realized she had everyone's attention. "Sorry. Did I miss something?"

"We're all waiting to hear what you've come up with for Operation Valentine." Dottie grinned.

"Oh. I do have something. I'll give you what I wrote for the arriving guests, and you can read it while I eat. Hold on a sec." She took her plate with her when she left the room and handed Dottie a sheet of paper upon her return.

Clearing her throat, Dottie read:

> *It's 1910 and you're undercover, investigating alleged illegal activity at Leopold Burk's residence. Invitations to his exclusive house parties are highly sought after, but your date managed to use family connections to get you invited to his annual Valentine's soirée.*

Keeping those connections a secret is imperative. When you arrive, gather with the other guests in the kitchen for hors d'oeuvres. The undercover waiter will leave your first clue in a crunchy snack.

She looked up and smiled. "There's a map and a list of other clues on here too. This is great, Lizzy. At the end, everyone will find a table piled with winners' gifts and a banner that says congratulations and invites them back to the kitchen for more snacks."

"We'll need supplies and volunteers to help during the event," Lizzy said.

"What kind of supplies?" Mrs. Jacobs asked. "If it's supposed to be 1910, do we need period costumes?" She looked over the narrow spectacles perched on the end of her nose with pursed lips.

"We have some from that play we did two years ago, but I don't think it's necessary except for a couple of volunteers maybe. What do you think, Lizzy?"

"How easy do you want to make it? The actors will be easier to spot if they're dressed differently."

"True. We can decide that later. As for supplies"—Dottie looked at the sheet of paper she held—"we'll need fortune cookies with a clue inside, red lipstick, a still and a barrel, a monocle, several printed clues, the winner's banner, and small wrapped gifts of some sort. We need to decide on the gifts and the hors d'oeuvres. Should we make them or have catering?"

"It would be cheaper to make them. Are we charging an entrance fee?" Stacy asked.

"Yes, I think that would be best. To cover costs." Dottie said. "How about five dollars a person?"

"Will that cover it? We have no idea how many people will come. Can we sell tickets in advance?" Stacy popped a bubble, reminding Lizzy of the great hair fiasco before Christmas. A hairdresser, Stacy had unwisely sabotaged Lizzy's hair in a fit of jealousy.

She had changed a lot since then. Happily dating Coral, her '80s hair wasn't quite as big, and her tops were slightly less scandalous.

"We don't want the price to prevent people from coming," Dottie said. "Let's make the food ourselves, and we can make more for the second day if we underestimate attendance."

"Make some of these quiches," Lizzy said as she helped herself to another. "I was researching small items we could buy in bulk for the prizes. They don't have to be very expensive. We could have tiny treasure boxes with chocolate coins inside. Or we could get magnets or stickers. Someone could even write a small historical booklet, and we could sell advertising at the end to offset the price of printing."

"Let's save that idea for next year. We don't have a lot of time." Mrs. Fickle snuck Mavis a piece of quiche.

Little stinker. That's why she's being so quiet. I wonder where the cats are.

"If there are no more questions, we'll adjourn for now. I'll order supplies, and we'll get together again to set everything up," Dottie said. "When can we expect Holly?"

"I'm not sure. She was supposed to be back today, but I don't know how she'll get here from the airport." *Why is everyone staring at me again? Like they know something I don't. I hate it when they do this.*

⁘⟞⟨⟩⟞⁘

After the raucous day, the house felt unnaturally quiet when her final guest left. Even Mavis was silent. "Where are the cats?" Lizzy asked, looking into big brown innocent-looking eyes. "You're not fooling me. What's going on?"

Mavis didn't move other than two thumps of her tail.

"Hmm. I guess we'd better find them." From her brief experience, she knew the difficulty of finding a cat who was scared or hiding. Her large house had a surprising number of niches and nooks seemingly designed for feline disappearances. Mavis trailed behind as she looked under furniture and inside cupboards, calling them.

After she searched all three floors, she returned downstairs and heard Candy's high-pitched meow. Mavis sat in front of the closed bathroom door.

Inside, Lizzy found Marmalade sleeping on the soft toilet-seat cover and Candy sitting on the bathmat. "How did you two get locked in here?" She ran a hand through her riotous hair and recoiled at the sweet scent of a noxious perfume. "Who would do that?"

Thinking back to when she last saw the cats and who was present, she had her first feelings of unease. Candy ran to Mavis and rubbed against her.

"Come on, let's go sit by the fire." Lizzy expected Marmalade to object when she picked her up, but she snuggled against her and purred. "You are full of surprises."

As they dozed in front of the fire, Lizzy contemplated the cat lying against her chest and her complete disinterest in Madeline. *I'll have to ask Holly about this. I wonder when she'll be back.* She had tried to call, but the phone went to voice mail. *I hope she's okay.*

Jolting awake at the sound of the doorbell and Mavis' barking, Lizzy disturbed Marmalade, who meowed dolefully. "I'm sorry, sweetheart. You go back to sleep." She laid her on the sofa and strode to the door.

"Who is it?"

"Jason. Did you forget about dinner?"

"I guess I did," she said as she opened the door for him. "I must have fallen asleep."

Jason glanced into the living area. "Looks like you weren't the only one."

"We had a busy day. Come on into the kitchen and tell me about Mr. Prichard while I find us something to eat."

Mavis, suddenly alert, danced behind them.

"What time is it anyway?"

"About five thirty."

"Mavis napped right past her dinner time." She turned to look at the little dog and laughed when she saw the cats sitting patiently next to the pantry door. "Cats are so interesting," she told Jason. "Candy's changing since Marmalade arrived. Speaking of which, have you heard from Holly?"

"I think she wants to surprise you."

"Oh. I was expecting her today."

Jason smiled.

Once Lizzy had refereed mealtime for her furry companions, she opened the freezer and pulled out one of the larger Tupperware containers.

"What's that?"

"I don't know. When Holly was giving me cooking lessons, we'd eat whatever we made for dinner, and I froze the rest. She told me to label them, but I forgot. It's probably tasty since she helped. Tell me about your rescue operation." Lizzy put the container in the microwave and sat down at the table.

"Well, Bart came with some of his buddies."

"The wood guy?"

"He actually runs a tree-removal service. He couldn't get his truck through, but he set up a pulley system and used tarps and ropes to make sure the rest of the tree didn't fall through the roof. Byron had a makeshift stretcher that he and some of his team took through the house to the attic; then they shielded Prichard while Bart and his team raised the heavy branches so they could get him out. It sounds simple, but it was dangerous, so they moved painfully slow. Prichard isn't a patient guy, and everyone was irritated with him by the time they got him out."

The microwave dinged.

"You said he was really lucky."

"He was. The chainsaw he was using shut itself off when it fell, and the branch missed his head. The floor was damaged but didn't give way. I don't think he even broke any bones."

He looked toward the microwave. "Did I hear a ding?"

"Yes." Lizzy stood. "Did you hear about the altercation over here?"

Chapter 7

Holly's Return

I cy wind cut through Holly's new Florida outfit, causing a violent shiver. She remembered hearing someone say that there was no such thing as bad weather, just bad clothing, and she was inclined to agree. Unfortunately, her heavy winter clothing was packed in one of her suitcases, and she'd have to retrieve them from the carousel before she could change.

Why is everyone moving so slow?

Her teeth began to chatter as she crossed the tarmac. Once inside, she stopped briefly at a kiosk for a hot cup of coffee, wrapping her frozen hands around it and blowing on the top before taking a warming sip.

She didn't see Jason in the arrival area, so she sat to wait for her suitcases to show up on the carousel. Sipping her coffee and thinking about her trip, she was startled by a hand on her shoulder.

"I almost didn't recognize you," Barker said.

"Oh, hi. Jason didn't tell me you were coming."

"We've had an eventful day. You look beautiful, but I hope you have a coat. We have to ride part way on a snowmobile."

"My winter clothes are in my luggage, but how will I get it home?"

"We can drop it off at the station here before we head back. I imagine Jason told you about the blizzard."

"Yeah. How's Lizzy doing?"

"I've only seen her a couple of times, but she seemed in good spirits. Show me which suitcase is yours, and I'll grab it for you."

She glanced at the carousel and saw one of her bags go by. "We just missed one."

"How many do you have?"

"Two. I needed one just for my winter gear."

"Well, let's get over there and catch the second." He grinned, and Holly felt like she was seeing him for the first time. He had been around for years, but he was always serious and circumspect in his uniform. "What's your first name, Barker?"

Dark blue eyes shining, he said, "Steve. No one calls me that because Doc Steve was here first."

His light brown hair was cut short, and his patrician nose commanded attention, but somehow it all worked. "There." Holly pointed. "The red one."

Barker leaned over and grasped the suitcase with a long arm.

"And here comes the other. That one."

Once they had retrieved both suitcases, Barker asked, "So what's the plan?"

"I'll take one in the restroom and change. Can you watch the other?"

"Yeah. Put anything you need with you in your backpack, and someone will return for the rest once the roads are clear."

"Thanks. I'll be right back." She wheeled the black suitcase to the ladies' room and set it on the counter to open it. Her snowsuit, long johns, hat, gloves, scarf, and boots were neatly awaiting her on top. Underneath, she had packed her toiletries and souvenirs, so she transferred those to her backpack, exchanging them with the change of clothes she always carried with her. Lose your luggage once and you take precautions. Changing in the ladies' room was awkward, but there was no way she was getting on the back of a snowmobile in her lightweight yellow dress.

⸎

Bundled from head to toe, Holly felt much better by the time she got into the taxi with Barker. They dropped off her luggage and rode to the lot where he had parked the snowmobile.

Grateful that his back shielded her from the wind, Holly felt the frigid gusts in her bones despite her warm clothing. *Amazing how quickly you can forget. Just a couple of weeks ago, this weather was normal. Now it feels wicked.* She wrapped her arms more tightly around Barker's waist and pressed her face against his broad back.

She looked up when Barker slowed. Her own home was shrouded in darkness, but catty-corner, Lizzy's lights shone cheerfully through her front curtains. "Can you drop me at Lizzy's?"

"That was my plan. Jason's waiting for me." He parked at the curb and helped her off the snowmobile. "Would you like an arm?" He held his out.

"Yes, please." She could hardly contain herself as she waited for Lizzy to answer the door. She heard Mavis first, then the door opened and there was her dearest friend. She threw her arms around Lizzy's neck and burst into tears.

"You're back! Don't do that. You'll make me cry too. Come on in and let me take your coat. You too, Barker. Jason's in the kitchen. Are you hungry?"

Laughing merrily, Holly asked, "What did you make?"

"*We* made mac and cheese before you left. I just defrosted it."

"I'd love some. Where's Candy?"

"In front of the fire, I think. Get comfortable in there, and I'll bring you a blanket and some tea."

"I'll come too," Barker said.

They walked into the living area, and Holly gasped. "Who's that?" She pointed at the large orange-and-white mound in front of the fire. "That can't be Candy. She was this big when I left."

Barker laughed and strode over to Marmalade, picking up the tiny ball of fluff curled up against her and carrying her to Holly. "That's the neighbors' cat. I'm sure Lizzy will tell you all about it." He sat next to her and turned to take a blanket Lizzy handed him, carefully wrapping it around Holly's shoulders. Without thinking, she leaned against him as she snuggled with her kitten.

Lizzy carried a tea tray into the living area followed by Jason carrying plates of mac and cheese. Holly smiled at her brother, surprised when his eyebrows rose slightly. Then she realized she looked pretty cozy with Barker and sat up straight. "It's so nice to be warm again."

"Have some tea and some warm food. That'll help."

"I see Mavis hasn't changed." Holly reached down and stroked her ears.

"You should have seen Holly's face when she came in here and saw Marmalade," Barker grinned.

"I completely forgot about that," Lizzy said. "I have so much to tell you."

"I have lots to tell you too."

"Can you stay over? Your house is probably freezing."

"Yes! Maybe I'll stay here indefinitely. I don't want to go out in that cold. How have you managed moving here in the middle of winter?"

"It wasn't quite as cold when I got here, and you helped me a lot."

"Eat up, Barker, then we should be on our way," Jason said. "We still have work to do."

"If you stop by tomorrow, I'll make you some cookies," Holly said, gratified by the sudden sparkle in his eyes.

"What time? I'll be here."

"Not too early unless Lizzy wants to bake tonight."

"Sure. Why not? Then we'll have something to munch on while we catch up."

"Do I get cookies too?" Jason asked.

"I'll make a double batch."

The men took their leave, everyone insisting Holly stay where she was. "Thank you for getting me home, Steve."

Jason's eyebrows rose higher that time.

"My pleasure," Barker said. "See you tomorrow."

Lizzy returned to find Holly with a dreamy little smile on her face. "What's going on with you and Barker?"

"Hm?" Holly glanced in her direction.

"You and Barker. When did that happen?"

"Nothing happened."

"Something did, because the two of you were acting… not lovey-dovey exactly, but different. Aware maybe."

"I never really noticed him before. He's very nice, isn't he?"

"He is. Yes. I like him a lot."

"Not like that." Lizzy caught Holly's worried look. "Just I like him as a person. Let me know when you're ready to make those cookies. Want a pair of slippers?"

"That would be great. I don't know how I got such a chill. I don't want to leave the fire yet."

"No hurry, except I want to eat cookies."

"Tell me about the cat. I thought you didn't like cats."

"I never said I don't like them. I just didn't know anything about them. I've learned a lot. I do have a question about this one though."

Holly tilted her head and waited.

"I guess I should start at the beginning. Mrs. Crocker left her house to her brother, and he's a piece of work." Lizzy told Holly about the tree and rescuing the cat. Then she told her about Madeline's visit, Mr. Prichard's accident, and the fight in her kitchen.

Eyes round, Holly asked who Madeline was fighting with.

"A lady named Christine. I guess she's an old friend of yours?"

"Not Christine Luc?"

"I don't know. She's tall and curvy with long blonde hair and a lot of makeup. She didn't know you're a vet, so I guess you haven't seen each other in a long time."

"Ugh. We were childhood friends, but she turned into such a bully. How does she know Mrs. Prichard?"

Lizzy shrugged. "My question is about Marmalade. She completely ignored Madeline when Rice brought her to visit, and I thought she was just really independent; unfriendly, I guess. But earlier today I found her and Candy locked in the bathroom, and when I picked her up, she snuggled against me and purred. She stayed on the sofa with me for a long time." Her brow furrowed as she thought. "I don't know much about cats, but that seems strange. Why would she act like that?"

"What do you mean by ignored? What did she do?"

"Well, Madeline called to her, and she opened one eye, then closed it. And when she knelt by the cat bed and petted her, she didn't move. She didn't hiss or anything. She just seemed to tolerate her. It was weird."

"Hmm." Holly studied the cat, then handed Candy to Lizzy and slid off the sofa, crawling toward her. "Hello, beautiful." She reached out a hand for Marmalade to sniff.

Lifting her head and gazing at Holly, the cat purred and rubbed her cheek against Holly's hand.

"Aren't you a sweet kitty."

"She loves being brushed." Lizzy watched as Marmalade rose and rubbed against Holly with her tail raised. Holly sat crosslegged, and within thirty seconds, the cat was in her lap.

"See what I mean?"

Playing with the cat's ears and running her hand along her tail, Holly looked up at Lizzy. "Based on her reaction to me, it seems she doesn't like Mrs. Prichard for some reason. She's probably not afraid of her, since she didn't hiss or run away."

"Do you think Marmalade might not be her cat?"

"That's hard to say, but she's friendly with me and she's not my cat either. Why didn't Mrs. Prichard take her?"

"She said the hotel has a no-pet policy."

"Untrue. Mr. Sanders loves animals. He fosters and rehomes strays around town." She gave Marmalade a little kiss and placed her back in her bed before rising.

"I'm finally getting too warm in front of this fire. I should take off my snowsuit before we bake."

"You can change in the bathroom or upstairs. I'm afraid Marmalade has moved into your room."

"I can share. I'll be right back."

Chapter 8

The Big Thaw

The two friends were up late, baking and sharing stories. Holly twisted her waist-long hair into a fantastical bun and wore Lizzy's ASPIRING COOK apron. Mavis was underfoot, and Holly was enchanted by Candy's antics. "I wish I hadn't left when she was so little. She's already grown so much. She's almost regular kitten-size."

Lizzy understood. Candy had lost her mother at birth, and they'd fed her with an eyedropper. She had been the size of a gerbil. She was still small, but her weight had doubled. "Are those cookies ready yet?"

Holly giggled and retrieved the first tray from the oven. "Hold your horses. They'll need to cool for a minute."

Mavis whined and groaned as if she hadn't been fed for a week. "I know, puppy. They smell so good." Warm cinnamon and sugar wafted through the kitchen. Closing her eyes and breathing deeply, Lizzy thought she might swoon. "By the way, I forgot to tell you about Dottie's latest brainchild."

"Uh-oh. Did she get you involved?"

"Not only that, but you're involved too." Lizzy explained the project, keeping one eye on the cookies.

"They made you come up with the scenario? And that's why everyone was over here yesterday?"

"That, and half the town came to rescue Mr. Prichard."

Placing a plate piled high with snickerdoodles on the table, Holly sat across from Lizzy. "You know, I enjoyed my trip, but once the conference was over, I was lonely. There's something special about Harperstown. It's not just knowing everyone—that can get annoying, actually."

"I know what you mean. This town is really active for how small it is. And you're always included in everything that's going on whether you want to be or not."

"Something like that. Being part of the community. In Florida I was just another random stranger. No one knew me. No one spoke to me. I felt invisible."

Lizzy studied her friend for a moment. "I was used to being ignored. I hated all the attention and scrutiny when I got famous. I just wanted to run away and hide."

"That didn't work too well, did it?"

"I'm glad it didn't. I was wrong."

The oven dinged, heralding a new batch of cookies.

⁕

Waking to the smell of bacon instead of Mavis' cold nose, Lizzy felt disoriented. Then she remembered Holly was back, and she smiled. She knew where Mavis was. Where there was food, there was dachshund. She turned to find Marmalade curled up against her back. "You're the least fickle, aren't you." She stroked the thick, fluffy fur and marveled at its softness. "I wish I could keep you."

Holly popped her head through the doorway, Candy perched on her shoulder. "Ready for breakfast?"

"Absolutely. I haven't had bacon since you left."

"Come on down. I have another surprise for you too."

Food on her mind, Lizzy threw on her clothes and ran downstairs. "Look outside," Holly said.

Lizzy didn't understand immediately, but then she noticed the three-foot-tall walls of snow on either side of the street and neighbors outside shoveling their walkways.

"The plows were able to get through," Holly said gleefully. "Just in time for my return."

"How?"

"It's supposed to get up to thirty-eight degrees today. After breakfast, I want to go turn my heater on. It'll take a while to heat the castle."

Lizzy loved Holly's house. The interior was decorated like a modern medieval castle, with stone walls, sconces, and a doorbell that sounded like a gong.

"When are you going to reopen the clinic?" she asked.

"It'll be officially open on Monday, but everyone knows I'm back."

Lizzy opened her mouth to ask, and Holly giggled. "Don't ask how. They just know. Come eat breakfast."

Busy sniffing the kitchen floor and looking up at the counter, Mavis stopped to watch Holly when she reappeared. She barked twice and whined.

"Why isn't she talking?" Holly placed Candy on the floor and carried two plates to the table.

"I don't know. Maybe it has something to do with the cats. She hasn't been getting my undivided attention lately."

"Poor puppy. You need some bacon and eggs, don't you."

"Aurooerer."

"Holly. I'm shocked." Lizzy watched her spoon some eggs and crumbled bacon into Mavis' bowl.

"I know. I know. But every rule needs to be broken once in a while, and she needs to know she's still top dog. Right, Mavis?"

Staring at her intently, Mavis thumped her tail twice and waited.

"Here you go." Holly placed the bowl on the floor, and Mavis quickly inhaled her offering, then stared at her some more, licking her snout. "No, that's it for now. It's our turn."

"I can hardly wait to get outside," Lizzy said. "Do you think the snow will melt?"

"No. It'll freeze up again tonight. At least the shops will open, and we'll be able to get around though. If it melts too quickly, we'll have other problems."

"Has that happened before?"

"You've noticed how all our porches are raised? Ever wonder why? I have a rowboat hanging in my garage."

As soon as the roads were clear, Jason drove to the shared rural hospital to interview Napoleon Prichard. He consulted with the nurse on duty before entering Mr. Prichard's room.

Wearing a hospital gown and sporting a thick growth of stubble and a bedhead, Mr. Prichard asked, "Why are you here?"

"You must be feeling better. Perhaps I should introduce myself. I'm Captain Jason Schneider of the Harperstown police department."

"Damn busybody if you ask me."

"I took an oath to protect and serve. May I ask why you decided to climb up on your icy roof when it was already unstable?"

"Mad—my wife, Madeline—took it into her head to blame me for the damage to our house, and she wouldn't let it go. I don't know what got into her. She's usually so reasonable. But nag, nag, nag. She was at me day and night. 'Why did we have to move here? Why did you have to cut down that tree? How could you wreck everything?' I couldn't stand it anymore. I had to do something. I thought I'd start by cutting the branches and removing them little by little. I don't know what happened. One minute I was sawing through a branch, and the next I was falling. I tried to stop myself. I grabbed the branch, but it went down with me." He shook his head.

"The doctors say you were incredibly lucky. Are you planning to go up there again?"

"I'll have to. The damage will be twice as bad when we have a thaw."

"I recommend getting some help or at least using some safety ropes."

"What do you know? I'm a contractor. I think I can cut down a tree."

Jason couldn't believe his ears. He pulled a chair close to Napoleon's bed and sat down. "Mr. Prichard, your track record isn't looking too good. Please take precautions if you insist on doing everything yourself."

"Yeah, yeah," he grumbled.

"One last question. How do you know Christine Luc?"

Napoleon opened his mouth, shut it again, and frowned. "Why would you ask me about her?"

"You first."

"She's involved with a business connection. Why?"

"Did you know she's from Harperstown?"

"No. I don't really know her." Napoleon stared at Jason.

"She and your wife had an altercation at your neighbor's house."

"What's that mean? An argument? How would they even know each other?"

"It was more than an argument, and your wife accused Christine of being a homewrecker."

Napoleon shook his head. "I don't know what's gotten into that woman. It's like she's turned into someone else."

"So you didn't have an affair, or a flirtation, with Christine?"

"Of course not. Lucian would've killed me."

Where have I heard that name before? "Lucian Basile? Mrs. Fickle's cousin?"

"Who's Mrs. Fickle?"

"Never mind. Is he in town too?"

"I hope not. I thought we squared things. But he might be if Christine's here."

Jason thought he looked worried. "Why would your wife think you were having an affair with Christine?"

"Lucian sometimes asked me to entertain her while he was conducting business. Someone we knew must have seen us.

"That's the only thing I can think of."

"I see. Well, thank you for your time." Jason stood. "Take care of yourself."

They shook hands, and Jason turned to leave.

"If I wanted to get some help with that tree," Napoleon asked, "do you know someone who wouldn't overcharge me?"

"I do." Jason stopped in his tracks. "One of the guys who helped get you out yesterday is an expert and very reasonable. I'll get you his card if you like."

By two o'clock, the snow was melting fast. Lizzy and Holly attempted to take Mavis on a walk but ended up pulling her on a sled. Their boots sank in deep slush that rose over the tops and dripped inside.

"My socks are wet, and my feet are frozen," Lizzy complained.

"That's why I have—these!" Holly pulled a pair of fuzzy orange socks out of her coat pocket and grinned. "Guess what else I have?"

"What?"

Like a magician, Holly pulled out a similar pair of socks from her other pocket. "I have a pair for you!"

"You really are the best. I was picturing myself squishing across Mrs. Fickle's pristine floor in my slushy socks."

"This is not the first time this has happened. I suspected we might end up with wet feet. If I had to take a guess, I'd say Mrs. Fickle has some warm slippers and a pot of tea waiting for us too."

That was all the encouragement Lizzy needed. She picked up her pace as they rounded the final corner and headed for the Fickle house. Dottie's husband Steve had shoveled the front walk and was working on the driveway. His face was pink with exertion and his long white beard shimmered in the sunlight. "Afternoon, ladies,"

"Hi, Doc," Holly said.

"Good afternoon," Lizzy added.

"Dottie's already inside. I'll come in for something warm to drink when I'm done."

Chapter 9

Setting the Scene

Mrs. Fickle greeted them at the door. "I'm so glad you came. And you brought Mavis. How wonderful. Get yourselves some nice warm slippers and join us in the sitting room. Steve lit the fire, and I brewed some tea."

Holly glanced at Lizzy and winked.

Lizzy had been to the Fickles' house once, before Christmas, but she had been too overwhelmed by the size and the opulent decorations to take in the details. She remembered wondering how Mrs. Fickle took care of such an enormous house by herself along with cooking and gardening and keeping an eye on her neighbors. *I'll have to ask Holly about that.* She accepted a cup of tea and ogled the pastries and finger sandwiches laid out on trays.

Dottie the mind reader said, "Help yourself to snacks. It's about dinner time so I thought we might all be hungry."

Mavis barked and wagged her tail.

"I love you, Dottie." Lizzy grinned and picked up a cucumber finger sandwich, giving a little piece to Mavis. "What's our plan today?"

"We thought you could walk us through the route you came up with and discuss details, to see if we need to make any changes," Dottie said.

"Good idea. Without seeing the places along the route, it's kind of theoretical."

"Great. Let's eat and get warmed up, and then we'll get started. Sage, thank you again for letting us use your house."

"Are you sure you want everyone to know about the secret passages and everything?" Lizzy asked.

"I've made some changes to how they usually appear, and I locked away my valuables. Plus, I finally got a burglar alarm after what happened last Christmas."

"Just having it helps, don't you think?" Lizzy asked. "I don't even use mine all the time, but knowing it's there makes me feel safer."

"Your intruders are locked up too." Dottie grinned.

"There is that." Lizzy laughed.

They snacked and peppered Holly with questions about her vacation, and then Dottie stood and clapped her hands. "Everybody ready to take the mystery tour? Let's start at the front door. I made three copies of Lizzy's introduction. We can use them to make notes."

As they worked their way through the house, they made small adjustments and ironed out details. The biggest change was the still in the basement. "Our guests should understand the significance of the still, and they should have to figure out a puzzle or something before they can proceed," Holly said.

"Do you have any ideas?" Lizzy asked. "I had thought they could pour themselves a little drink, but we don't want small children getting bombed at a community event."

"A very good point." Mrs. Fickle laughed. "There's a lazy waiter in the wall over there. We could have people send a bottle upstairs and wait for it to return with a message."

"We'll need a lot of bottles though."

"How about they send a full bottle upstairs and take the empty to a crate by the still?" Lizzy said.

"The still could be filled with fizzy water, and they have to fill the bottle before they send it up," Holly suggested.

"Small bottles then. Will the guests understand what's going on from the context?" Dottie asked.

They all agreed it was likely. The secret passages were slightly different than Lizzy had pictured, so they had to be fleshed out as well, and the prize room was not what she imagined at all.

"This is kind of creepy," she said when they entered.

"Your idea was excellent though," Mrs. Fickle said. "I still have some of the original gaming tables in storage. If we place them around the room and set up a bar, the guests will be able to see what the homeowner was hiding. Then the gift table can be placed along the back wall."

"How will people be able to get out?" Lizzy asked.

"They'll have to go back through the secret passage, but then we can funnel them down the main stairs."

"It might create a serious bottleneck. We don't want any accidents," Holly said.

"Let's have a volunteer controlling traffic. Maybe they can request a secret password," Dottie said. "*Queen of Hearts*. Once we get everything set up and decide on staff, we'll need someone to test it. I nominate Steve. Let's walk the route back to try it out."

On returning to the ground floor, Lizzy looked around for Mavis. *She's being awfully quiet.* "Have we decided on prizes?" she asked distractedly.

"I found something I think is good." Dottie took out her phone and pulled up an image of a small metal replica of a roulette wheel on a key chain. "They're under five dollars if you order in bulk, and Harperstown Realty agreed to pay the extra fee to put their logo on the back. Best yet, they can get here in time for the event. What do you think?"

"We'll have to make a huge guess on the quantity," Lizzy said.

"Carl said Harperstown Realty will purchase any leftovers for promotional gifts, so we can order in bulk and save money. I suggest two thousand."

"That's a lot. We only have 768 people in the whole town."

"But we're advertising in Sioux Falls as well. We want to get as many guests as we can."

"How can we wrap that many?" Holly asked. "That will take days."

"We'll get little gift bags. We can do it."

Heads turned toward a clamor in the sitting room. Lizzy took off at a sprint, the others trotting behind her. Mavis stood on the coffee table, wolfing down finger sandwiches and pastries indiscriminately. Two of the silver trays lay on the floor, surrounded by whatever the little dog hadn't managed to consume.

"Mavis!"

Mavis looked toward Lizzy and licked her snout. Then she started gobbling even faster, before Lizzy could reach her.

Dottie and Mrs. Fickle laughed, and Holly shook her head. "That naughty puppy is going to have a tummy ache."

They all helped clean up the sitting room and decided on the date and purpose of their next meeting before disbanding. Lizzy pulled the slightly heavier sled on her walk home with Holly. When they rounded the corner, Barker stood leaning against his cruiser, waiting for them.

***

Engaged in conversation with Lizzy, Holly didn't notice him right away, but when she did, her pulse rate rose and she thought she was probably blushing.

"I'm here for those cookies you promised me." His smile lit up his face.

"What cookies?"

"You forgot about them?"

"Are you kidding?" Lizzy asked. "She made dozens. Although I might have eaten a few."

"A few." Holly scoffed. "A few dozen maybe."

"Hey, you were eating them too. Come on in, Barker." Lizzy unlocked the door and hefted a sleeping Mavis from the sled. Marmalade and Candy ran to greet them, the large tabby rubbing against Lizzy's legs and the kitten trying to climb her pant leg.

They all removed their boots and peeled off their outerwear before heading for the kitchen. "Hold on a second, and I'll light the fire and put Mavis to bed. You can tell Barker about Mavis' food fest."

Holly hooked her arm around his and led him into the kitchen, telling him all about their luncheon meeting at the Fickle house. He was still chuckling when she placed a plate of cookies on the table and invited him to have a seat. "What would you like to drink?" she asked.

"Milk and cookies go well together. Or hot chocolate."

"Let's see." She looked in the refrigerator. "I don't think she has milk."

She turned and hollered, "Lizzy."

"I'm right here." Lizzy entered the kitchen. "What is it?"

"Steve said he'd like milk or hot chocolate. Do you have either of those?"

"I have half and half or those little packets of hot chocolate mix. Will one of those do?"

"Anything's okay. Really."

"Coffee with half and half?"

"Sure." He smiled. "May I have a cookie?"

"Of course. Help yourself." Holly sat next to him. "These are the chocolate chip, these are snickerdoodles, and these are pfeffernusse."

Barker took a pfeffernusse first. "My mother used to make these. Very nostalgic." He bit into it, creating a dusting of powdered sugar down the front of his uniform. "I might need a bib," he mumbled around the cookie.

Holly popped out of her chair to grab a tea towel, then carefully brushed the sugar off his shirt front. "Pros and cons." She smiled.

Chapter 10

Dress Rehearsal

The first annual Harperstown Mystery Maze was scheduled for the weekend before Valentine's Day. All the volunteers assembled at the Fickle house the day before for a final dress rehearsal. Dr. Steve, the elected guinea pig, waited on the porch while his wife Dottie and Sage Fickle rearranged the entrance. Rubber mats ran from the entry to the first room on the left, where coat racks were available. Guests were to leave their coats and boots there and proceed farther down the hall to the kitchen. Lizzy would accompany Doc Steve through the house to observe his reactions.

Mrs. Fickle finally opened the door and greeted Steve. She handed him a flyer and told him where to leave his coat. Lizzy watched him remove his outerwear and read the scenario. Then he left the coat room and glanced around. "Will people be able to find the kitchen?" he asked. "You might want to let the guests know where it is."

"Noted," Mrs. Fickle said. "It's farther down the hall on the left."

Steve walked into the kitchen, where several people were talking and snacking on hors d'oeuvres. Greeting the others, he looked at his flyer again before examining the snacks on the table. "A crunchy cookie," he mumbled to himself. "Am I allowed to eat while I'm in here?" he asked Lizzy.

"Of course. And after you've finished the maze as well."

He took a finger sandwich and wandered over to the tray of fortune cookies. "Did they have these in 1910?"

"Not exactly like these." Lizzy smiled.

Selecting one, Steve pulled out the paper inside and read, "Follow the lady in red stilettoes."

He looked around at other people's feet. Everyone was wearing socks, so he left the kitchen and watched for someone in red heels.

Holly walked from one end of the hall to the other, her red shoes *clack-clacking* on the wooden floor. Veering toward a single door, she entered, exited, and walked back down the hall.

Steve watched her pass by twice, then headed for the door. Inside the half bath, a message scrawled across the mirror in red lipstick read, "Look under the vase of roses."

Chuckling to himself, he looked in each room. There were several vases, but the next clue was under the coffee table in front of the fire. Marmalade hissed at him as he approached. Mavis climbed under the table with him and licked his nose. "Cut it out, you scallywag." Taped to the bottom of the table was a note. "Descend into darkness." He slid out from under the table and asked Lizzy, "Will everyone be able to get under there?"

"Hmm. I didn't think of that. Do you have any better ideas?"

"I did not say that." He laughed. "You are the creator. I was just thinking about certain folks who don't get around too well."

"The stairs could be a problem too if we're trying to accommodate everyone."

"True. Maybe make a note and confer with the others. Anyway, onward. 'Descend into darkness.' The basement, perhaps? Where might that be? Your guests might benefit from a simple map."

"We don't want to make it too easy."

"A sign on the door then? How will they ever find it?"

"Okay. A sign." Lizzy smiled. "Do you know where it is?"

"Under the staircase, I believe."

Lizzy nodded and went back to observing. *The moment of truth. Will he figure it out?*

Steve went down the dimly lit basement steps and headed toward the table in the middle of the room. The still and a crate of empty bottles sat on the table.

"Fill a bottle and send it upstairs," a sign read.

A red arrow on the floor and a glowing wall sconce next to the open dumbwaiter provided additional hints.

He filled a bottle and placed it in the dumbwaiter before pressing the button. Then he waited. The dumbwaiter wasn't quiet. Lizzy could hear it travel upward and stop. Then it began its descent. When it reopened, it contained an empty bottle and a note. "Watch the man with the monocle. Destroy this message."

Steve crumpled the note and placed it in his pocket, then returned upstairs.

Volunteers were milling about, so he stood and watched them. Dave walked by wearing a monocle. He walked past the basement door, into the dining room, then back toward the library.

Steve followed him and watched as he adjusted a note between two books. He left, and Steve approached the books and took out the note. "Pull out the red book."

Swinging his head from side to side, he spotted one red book along the far wall of bookshelves. He stretched out his hand to take the book, and the bookshelf slid to the left, leaving a narrow opening in the wall.

"Whoa. That's cool." He poked his head inside. Dimly lit with electric lanterns, the short passage ended with stone steps leading upward to the second floor. On the back of the exit door, a note read, "Don't let the seamstress see you."

Raised voices met their ears as they exited. He glanced at Lizzy. "Is that part of the game?"

She shook her head. "Let's go check it out."

* * *

After Steve left the basement, Holly took a break and found a note taped to the bathroom mirror. "Come up to the sewing room ASAP. S," it read. She didn't know which *S* wrote the missive, but she chucked her heels and ran up the stairs.

As she approached the door to the sewing room, she heard Rice say, "I thought you and Holly were friends. Why would you say something like that?"

"Something like what? I didn't say anything."

Holly entered the room and stared. "Christine?"

"I have no idea what she's talking about. I swear."

"You're such a liar."

Tilting her head, Holly said, "We haven't seen each other in ten years. I don't know what you would even say about me."

Christine's voice rose. "Nothing. I didn't say anything."

"At least have the guts to say it to my face."

Lizzy and Steve burst through the door as Christine, her face red, launched herself at Holly. Shoving her glass at Holly, Rice got between them and assumed a defensive stance.

Steve grabbed Christine's raised fist. "What's going on here?"

They all began speaking at once.

"Stop!" Lizzy said. "We'll figure this out later. Everyone back to your posts. We're not finished." To Steve she said, "Let's go back to the passage and see if you can find the sewing room."

Holly set Rice's glass on the table and left the room with Lizzy and Steve, but she could still hear the other two squabbling.

Lizzy gave her a reassuring squeeze. "Don't worry. We'll talk about it at the meeting. Go get yourself some refreshments."

As she headed downstairs, Holly's mind was awhirl. *I don't understand either of them. What did Christine say, and why would she attack me? Why would Rice try to protect me?* Feeling tired and disheartened, she wished she could just go home.

⁂

Lizzy ran a hand through her hair, causing it to stand up straight. She led Steve back to the passage. "Now imagine we've just seen the sign and exited into this room. Where will we go next?"

"The clue said, 'Don't let the seamstress see you,' so I would probably go out into the hall first. Will the doors be open?"

"Yes."

"Then I'd walk down the hall and look into each room to see if I could find something like a sewing room."

"Okay. Let's go." She followed him down the hall.

They'd already been in the sewing room, but he did his due diligence, trying to imagine they hadn't. He observed Rice sitting at an old-fashioned sewing table where she alternately watched a closed door and read a book. Every few minutes, she rose and walked to the window, and the second time, Steve sprinted for the door.

Inside, there was an arrow pointing to the left and a note that read, "Turn the vase clockwise".

Following the passage, they came to another staircase with a door at the top. The door led to a closet-sized room that was completely empty except for a purple vase sitting atop a white end table. Steve rotated the vase as instructed, and the wall slid open.

Gaming tables and a bar populated the windowless room, and along one wall stood a table piled high with prizes in small pink gift bags. Above the table, a banner read CONGRATULATIONS.

Christine stood smiling behind the bar. "Welcome winners and congratulations. Please sign the book and take a gift, then make your way back to the kitchen for refreshments."

"Do I get a gift?" Steve asked.

"Sure. You completed the course. Our only potential problem is making sure no one gets hurt when all the guests are traveling up and down the final staircase. We may have someone asking for the password at the bottom and helping direct traffic."

"Are you serving drinks up here?"

"No. I have bottled water if anyone needs it."

"Thank you, Christine," Lizzy said. "Make sure everything's set up for tomorrow and we'll meet downstairs."

The sewing room was empty when they retraced their steps to the second floor. Lizzy pointed out an EXIT sign leading to the main staircase.

The entire group was assembled in the living room when Lizzy and Steve returned. "How did it go?" Dottie asked.

"I think we're about ready, but Steve had a few suggestions."

"He would." Dottie grinned.

"First, he suggested we include a simple map or at least label the door to the basement."

"Good idea. A sign, I think," Dottie said.

"He also thought some people might have difficulty getting under the coffee table. Does anyone know a child who could hang around in there and volunteer to look under the table?"

"Or maybe we could have a pile of papers lying on the floor under the table so people could just grab one," Mrs. Fickle suggested.

"That reminds me; we should make sure we have duplicate signs in case one gets damaged or goes missing," Lizzy said. "Whoever's doing the walk-through can make sure they're all there."

"What happens if the seamstress sees you?" Steve asked.

"She'll just tell you that door is private and direct you back out into the hall." Lizzy smiled. Then, scanning the room, she asked, "Where are Rice and Christine?"

"I haven't seen them since we started," Dottie said.

"We should probably reconsider our shift rotation. We have some personality conflicts and don't want any incidents during the event. Maybe Stacy and Holly can swap shifts. Then Rice and Coral can switch."

"Is that okay with you?" Dottie asked Stacy and Coral, who both nodded.

"Did Mavis behave herself this afternoon?"

"Oh yes. Such a sweet puppy."

"I hope she doesn't make herself sick with all her begging."

Chapter 11

The Best-Laid Plans

Making a final pass through the house, Lizzy looked down at Mavis and smiled. "Everything's perfect. Let's go tell Mrs. Fickle she can open the door."

"Ahrouerer." Mavis wagged her tail and looked at Lizzy expectantly.

"Come on." She strode to the front door where Mrs. Fickle, a pleasant smile on her face, perched on a barstool with a cashbox. "Ready?"

"Yes, dear. I'm feeling quite excited." Mavis disappeared under her long skirt, and she giggled.

Lizzy eyed her colorful sweater vest and scarf. "Will you be warm enough?"

"I believe so. Dottie said she'll bring me warm drinks and spell me when I need a break."

"Okay. Let the first few guests in, then wait a minute or two. We don't want everyone waiting too long, but we do need to space them out a bit." She watched as Mrs. Fickle opened the door and gasped. The line went down to the sidewalk, along the street, and disappeared around the corner. Cars were parked on both sides of the street.

Mrs. Fickle invited the first three couples inside and closed the door. Mavis poked her head from under the long skirt and barked as she collected tickets, handed each guest a flyer, and directed them to the coat room. As the third couple headed for the kitchen, she admitted one more.

"I'll be back," Lizzy said. "Come on, Mavis."

Warm and fragrant, the kitchen was filled with excited chatter and soft strains of jazz.

Mavis immediately ceased barking and began sniffing for crumbs. *Priorities*, Lizzy thought. She observed the first couple as they discovered their clue and went in search of the lady in red stilettoes. Mavis was uninterested in leaving the kitchen, so Lizzy asked Dottie to keep an eye on her.

Four hours in, Holly took over for Stacy, to save her feet. "I'll go up and check on Coral," Stacy said. "She might need a break."

Holly, focusing on the task at hand, didn't pay too much attention. She put on her red shoes and began traversing her character's route. The guests' enthusiasm was amusing, especially her disruptive young neighbors, who seemed to have forgotten they were indoors. Observing Chad and Ron, in their late teens, she hoped they wouldn't unduly disturb the other guests. She watched them enter the bathroom, then sprint by her into the sitting room. When they reemerged, they were laughing and shoving each other on their way to the basement door.

Several guests milled around the bathroom door, muttering to each other. When they caught sight of Holly, they gathered around her. "What's the clue in the bathroom supposed to mean? 'Go to hell?' Is that one of the rooms in the house?"

"What? No. That's not a clue." Holly hurriedly opened the bathroom door and stared in shock. "Just a moment please," she said.

Lizzy looped around the course, making sure guests found the clues and proceeded in the right direction. She ran into Stacy on the second floor, and they arrived in the sewing room to find Christine leaning in close behind Coral and giving her a back massage.

Stacy froze.

"Christine, why aren't you at your post?" Lizzy asked.

Both women turned, Christine with a sly smile and Coral sporting a worried frown.

"Come upstairs with me now."

"You're not the boss."

"Right now, I am. Get back to your post or you'll be replaced. Every time I see you, you're causing trouble."

"I was just—"

"Upstairs. Now."

The guests Lizzy had been trailing were already in the secret room. Two young men were yelling and throwing gifts from the table at each other. They stopped abruptly when Lizzy and Christine entered the room.

"Kindly take one prize and make your way back downstairs," Lizzy said. Then she turned to Christine. "Please clean up this mess, and I'll be back with Dottie."

"You'll be sorry," she heard Christine mutter as she left.

Mascara running from red eyes, Coral sat at the sewing table downstairs, staring at the door to the hall. Stacy was gone.

Lizzy walked down the main staircase to find Dottie. First, she found Holly, surrounded by a group of guests.

Eyes wide, Holly whispered, "Help. Stacy just stormed by and said she quit, and someone sabotaged the clue in the bathroom. We need to clean it off and get some more lipstick."

"Okay. Everyone. The correct clue is to look under the roses. I'll try to delay some of the guests behind you."

Holly followed Lizzy into the kitchen where she said, "Please take your time and have a few more snacks. We've had a small delay."

"Where's Dottie? She's supposed to be watching Mavis."

"Judging from the barking, I'm guessing she's that way." Holly giggled and pointed toward the front door.

Jason and Barker were third in line when Dottie made her apologies and closed the front door. "Is that bad?" Barker asked.

Removing his hat and running his gloved hand through his curls, Jason said, "I'm not sure. Maybe the guests are just moving slower than expected."

Five minutes later, screaming erupted inside. They pushed their way to the door, and Jason pounded on it with his fist. "Police. Open up," he shouted.

Holly opened the door. "Thank goodness." She sighed.

Guests were screaming about a rabid dog and running in all directions.

"Where's the dog?" Jason asked.

Holly pointed to Lizzy, who was holding Mavis and attempting to wipe what looked like blood from her snout.

"Everyone calm down," Jason commanded. "Please move quietly to the kitchen or the sitting room." He turned to Barker. "I need to have a meeting with the staff. Where's Mrs. Fickle?"

Dave rushed in. "I need help. We've had an accident in the secret passage."

"What kind of accident?" Barker asked.

"Someone broke the electric lights, and one of the guests tripped in the dark and hurt herself. She needs a doctor."

Dottie, that stoic and ever-optimistic bastion of self-control, dropped to the floor with her head in her hands. Holly sat next to her and put her arm around her shoulders.

"Barker, call Doc Steve and go with Dave," Jason said.

"The whole event seems to be unraveling," Lizzy said. "I think we're going to have to shut down, at least until we can regroup."

Jason ran his fingers along the edge of his chapped lips, then saw Lizzy staring and put his hands in his pockets. "Why don't I announce a two-hour break? We'll guide whoever's currently in the house toward the exit and have a meeting. First, show me what Mavis got into."

Lizzy led him into the coat room and held on to Mavis as she wriggled mightily to get down. The scene looked ghastly, globs of red on an otherwise pristine white fur coat. Evidence of Mavis' activity, especially the flurry of tiny paw prints, further muddied the scene. Jason squatted down, stuck a finger in the sticky red substance, and brought it to his nose. "Hmm. Strawberry," he said.

"Strawberry?"

"Jam. Yes. That's why Mavis likes it so much."

"Who would do that? It wasn't an accident. No one carries a jar of jam around and accidentally dumps it on someone's expensive coat. An animal activist?"

Jason closed the door behind them when they left the room and rubbed his dry lips again. "They might have wanted us to think so, but combined with the lights…"

"And the clue in the bathroom."

He looked sharply at Lizzy.

"Someone changed the clue."

"Is anyone missing?"

"Stacy quit. Rice isn't here yet. I think Coral and Christine are still upstairs, and Mrs. Fickle disappeared."

Shaking his head, Jason radioed Deputy Nettle for assistance. He escorted the guests from the kitchen and the sitting room outside, where he raised his voice and announced the temporary closure of the event.

As Jason escorted the guests toward the exit, Dottie stood and took a deep breath. "Let's go make some tea." Lizzy and Holly followed her into the kitchen, where they leaned against the counters in silence.

"We need a plan," Lizzy said finally. "I'll go upstairs and try to muster the stragglers. Maybe you two can help escort the last guests outside.

"Do you have any idea where Mrs. Fickle could be?" *I wonder if she took the basement passage. But why? What happened?*

Holly looked at Dottie, and they both shook their heads.

"Okay. I'll start at the top and work my way down." Lizzy handed Mavis to Holly and left the room. She climbed the stairs to the second floor and walked down the hall to the sewing room, where Coral remained sitting at her post.

"Have you seen Stacy?" Her voice shook.

"Holly said she quit and stormed out of the house. We've temporarily shut down the maze and are going to have a meeting downstairs, so if you can head down, that would be great."

"Now?"

"Yeah. I'll be down in a few." Lizzy went through the unmarked door and up the stairs to the secret room, entering and looking around. It was empty. The gifts from the prize table remained strewn across the carpet. *Strange. Where'd she go?*

She checked a few of the bedroom doors on her way down, but finding them open or locked, she continued back to the main floor. A commotion in the library caught her attention, and following the noise, she discovered Barker, Dave, and Dr. Steve attending to a woman from the committee who was evidently hurt. A familiar-looking portly man stood to one side, wringing his hands.

Observing from the doorway, Lizzy heard Barker address the man as Pastor Marshall, and she realized where she had seen him. *Mrs. Turnbull must be his wife.* Physically, they seemed an odd couple, but Lizzy could see clearly that they were well suited.

"I just wanted to show Marshall the maze. I was so proud of all the ladies' work." Looking up at Lizzy, Mrs. Turnbull said, "I hope I didn't ruin everything."

Lizzy smiled kindly at the tiny woman. "We're having some problems today, but they are in no way because of you. I'm very sorry about your accident." She looked at the doctor. "Will she be all right?"

"Yes. She has a sprained ankle and lacerations from the broken glass. I've called for an ambulance."

"Thank you, Doctor." Lizzy backed out of the room and decided to take the passage to her house in a final attempt to find Mrs. Fickle.

She exited her basement and looked around. Soft snoring emanated from the living area, where Mrs. Fickle and the cats sat in Lizzy's lavender recliner before a merrily burning fire. Not wanting to startle her, Lizzy perched on the edge of the coffee table and whispered, "Mrs. Fickle?" She waited a moment then said, "Sage."

Mrs. Fickle opened her eyes and blinked. "Oh. Hello, dear. I must have dozed off."

"Why did you leave? Are you okay?"

Stroking Marmalade with a tremulous hand, she said, "I was afraid. Lucian showed up. He's wandering around in my house. How will I know if he leaves?"

Lizzy thought the best way was to watch the door, but she said, "So you left Dottie at the door and came over here?"

Mrs. Fickle nodded.

"We've been having some trouble and had to close temporarily. Do you want to come back for the meeting?"

"I guess I should. May I sleep here tonight?"

"Yes, of course. And we can set your burglar alarm, so we'll know if anyone tries to get in or out of your house."

Mrs. Fickle rose, displacing Marmalade. "I love your sweet kitties. They're so comforting."

"Neither of them is actually mine, but I know what you mean. When we get back, where shall we say you've been?"

"Let's just say I was resting in one of the locked bedrooms."

Lizzy thought that was a reasonable explanation. She wrinkled her nose at a sickly-sweet smell and gave the still a cursory glance as they passed through Mrs. Fickle's basement. The light on the dumbwaiter glowed green, although the hatch was closed.

I'll have to check on that later.

When they exited the basement on the first floor, Rice was lurking in the hallway. *Oops. She could blow our story.* "When did you get here?" Lizzy asked.

"I don't know. A while ago."

"Did someone let you in? We locked the doors about half an hour ago."

"No, I got here before that."

That didn't make sense, but Lizzy let it go. "Have they started the meeting?"

"What meeting?"

Lizzy sighed. "In the sitting room. Come on."

Rice glanced back at the basement door but then followed.

Chapter 12

Second Try

Holly looked up when Lizzy entered with Mrs. Fickle and Rice. She was sitting very close to Barker and surreptitiously holding his hand. She knew Lizzy noticed when one eyebrow rose. Holly snickered to herself. Lizzy always noticed everything.

Standing in front of the fireplace with Mavis sniffing his boots, Jason asked, "Is everyone accounted for now?"

"Except Christine," Lizzy said.

"I wonder where she went," Coral said. "I didn't see her go by."

"You were a little preoccupied for a while," Rice said.

"How do you know?"

"Stacy told me."

"When did you—"

"Let's try to stay on topic," Lizzy said. "You didn't take any breaks?"

"I got Holly to cover for me when I did."

"All right." Jason took charge. "Let's go over everything that's happened and try to make a timeline. You have a guest book, right?"

"Yes. I have it here. We don't have times though," Dottie said.

Holly wasn't listening very carefully as Jason led them back through the incidents. She was watching Lizzy and wondering if she should tell her about Christine's bizarre behavior. She had seen Mrs. Fickle's cousin with Lizzy's neighbor too and wondered what they were doing together.

"Assuming the saboteur has left the house, I think you can probably reopen for the afternoon," Jason said. "Let me know if anything else occurs, and we'll continue investigating."

Dottie stood and began calling out names and their posts. "Lizzy, why don't you and Mavis take the sewing room? Holly, since you're the only one with red shoes, I'd like you to remain in the same position. Is that okay?"

"Yes."

"Someone needs to man the gift room until we find Christine. Can you do that, Rice?"

"I guess so. Can I kick her out when she comes back?"

"Tell her to come see me. Take up your posts. We'll reopen in ten minutes. And everyone—keep an eye out for anything out of the ordinary."

<hr>

Mavis hopped up the stairs behind Lizzy and Rice. "I forgot to ask if the lights in the secret passage were fixed," Lizzy said.

Rice paused with the unmarked door open but then continued on without responding.

She can be so strange sometimes. I never know what she's thinking. "Well, Mavis, we're supposed to pretend we don't see people go by. My guess is that you're going to give the show away."

Mavis barked once and wagged her tail.

Lizzy picked her up and sat at the table with her. She glanced at the first guest through the secret passage, then turned her back. Mavis barked, of course, so Lizzy petted her and said, "What are you barking at, puppy?"

The guests chuckled and scurried across the room to the unmarked door.

Two hours sped by, and Rice said she needed a break. Stacy had returned and apologized, so she took over on the first floor and Holly arrived upstairs to cover.

When it was time to close, Rice still hadn't returned. Holly joined Lizzy on the second floor and plopped on the extra chair.

Mavis sniffed her feet and howled, her legs stiff and the hair on her back standing on end.

"What's the matter puppy?" Holly tried to pick her up, but Mavis somehow made herself heavy and howled again.

"It's way past dinner time. Maybe that's it?" Picking her up, Lizzy said, "Come on. Let's get you something to eat."

Mavis struggled to get down, then gazed at her with big brown eyes and whined.

The volunteers did a double check for straggling guests and left together through the front door, where Mrs. Fickle carefully set her alarm.

Holly carried her small overnight bag, and Lizzy dressed Mavis in her harness and winter coat, allowing her to walk. The remaining slush refroze as the sun set, but Lizzy was getting better at remaining on her feet when she slid.

They walked around the corner and found Jason waiting with three boxes of pizza. "Where did you get those?" Lizzy asked with a grin.

"Even though Dave's been volunteering at the maze, the diner's still open. Barker said to save him some."

"Why don't we eat by the fire? I'll just feed Mavis and get some plates."

Mrs. Fickle remained in the living area while Jason built a fire. Holly followed Lizzy into the kitchen and watched as she prepared three bowls, then turned to call the cats. Already in the kitchen, of course, they sat in front of the refrigerator like statues.

Placing the cats' bowls down first, Lizzy finally gave Mavis hers, remembering the little doggy massage, but Mavis didn't eat. She stared at Lizzy and whined.

"What's wrong with her?"

"I don't know. Maybe she has a tummy ache from all the snacking she did today." Holly approached her to check, but Mavis lowered her head over her bowl and growled softly. "I guess she'll eat when she wants to."

Lizzy handed plates and napkins to Holly. "Go on in and get some pizza. I'll be there in a few minutes." Mavis stayed where she was, head lowered over her bowl, so Lizzy sat next to her on the floor. "What's going on? I've never seen you like this except when I was arrested. Does your tummy hurt?"

Mavis' head went up, and she began to bark. She ran to the front door, wagging her tail, and the doorbell rang.

Lizzy rose and followed in time to see Holly open the door for Barker.

Mavis, sniffing Holly's feet, resumed howling. Then she went and lay in her bed by the fire.

The pizza was cold. Lizzy was perplexed. After living with Mavis for two months, she thought she knew her well, but her behavior was baffling.

Doggy stairs at the foot of her bed and a new open-bedroom-door policy had greatly reduced Lizzy's sleep interruptions. That night, however, Mavis paced and whined. The *click, click, click* of her nails on the wooden floor and Mrs. Fickle's snoring weaved in and out of Lizzy's dreams.

At one point, she thought she heard alarm bells. She opened her eyes and listened intently, but the house was eerily silent. The sounds a large hundred-year-old house made were many and varied. The occasional silence was uncomfortable. As she drifted back to sleep, Lizzy heard sirens in the distance. She dreamt of a severed head in the dumbwaiter.

Mavis woke her at six, barking and nudging her with her cold nose. Lizzy groaned and threw her blankets aside. "I know. Hold on." She grabbed their coats and took Mavis outside, still in her pajamas. She was mortified to see Jason stride around the corner with his German shepherd, Harvey.

"Are you making a fashion statement?" he asked with a grin.

"You know better than that. She's done her business, so let's get inside." She bent to rub Harvey's ears. "Hello, Harvey. Mavis missed you."

"Is it safe to bring him in?"

"Holly took Candy home, and I think Marmalade is sleeping with Mrs. Fickle."

"Good. I need to talk to you."

"Want some coffee?"

"Yes, please." He sat at the table and watched as she started a pot of coffee and took some of Dottie's pastries out of the refrigerator. Mavis was watching too.

"I guess you've got your appetite back. Has Harvey eaten?"

"You'd better believe it. He never misses a meal."

After she fed Mavis, Lizzy sat across from Jason, trying to straighten out her bedhead with her fingers. "What's up?"

"Did you hear Mrs. Fickle's alarm last night?"

"It woke me, I think. When I listened for it though, it was gone. I thought I was dreaming. Did someone break in?"

"No. I think they were inside and set the alarm off when they came out."

"Why do you think that?"

"All the bedroom doors were open, and someone did a thorough search. They wouldn't have had time to do that if the alarm went off when they broke in. Also, the front door was unlocked and standing open, but there weren't any footprints inside."

"Do you know what they were looking for? Or if they took anything?" She rose and poured two cups of coffee.

"There's really no way of knowing unless Mrs. Fickle notices something missing. What time are you going back over?"

"Dottie said to be there at ten. We're not opening until eleven because of church."

"Are you going?"

She placed the cups on the table and resumed her seat. "To church?"

"Yeah. It's a good place to meet people."

"I don't know. I guess I could. How's Mrs. Turnbull?"

"She's fine. She might look fragile, but she's a force to be reckoned with."

On her feet as the deep bass of Harvey's bark preceded the loud thump of falling books, Lizzy sprinted from the kitchen, followed by Jason. Harvey was jumping against the bookshelves and barking. Marmalade crouched on top, hissing, her fur standing on end. Mrs. Fickle stood quivering on the stairs in her housecoat, her face puckered and her long hair a tangled mess. Mavis sat in her bed watching the drama unfold.

"Harvey, no!" Jason scolded.

"I'm so sorry. I didn't know he was here."

"Don't worry, Mrs. Fickle."

"Maybe you can take Harvey for a little walk while I get Marmalade settled down and fed. I'll pour you some warm coffee when you get back." Lizzy smiled at Jason.

"I still need to talk to Mrs. Fickle."

"She can get dressed while you're out."

Jason nodded. "Does Mavis want to come too? Come on, Harvey. Let's take a walk. Mavis!"

The little dog didn't respond immediately. She watched Jason get Harvey into his snow suit before trotting to the door, tail wagging. Lizzy helped get her dressed for the cold, and she left with Jason.

"I'll text you when Marmalade's safe in her room," Lizzy called after him.

Marmalade remained atop the bookshelves while Mrs. Fickle went upstairs to dress. In the kitchen, Lizzy poured food into the cat bowl and waited. "Aren't you hungry, sweet girl?" she called softly. Sitting with her coffee and a pastry, she whispered, "Come get your breakfast, Marmalade." She hoped she wouldn't have to get a ladder.

Alone in the kitchen, she let her thoughts flow freely. *This town. It's like quicksand. There's so much going on all the time, and I keep getting sucked in. Why does Jason want me to go to church? Is he going? Maybe Rachel can get involved with a church mystery in the next book. A crooked pastor? Someone drowned in the baptismal—what do you even call it? I'd have to do a lot of research.* That was okay with her. She liked learning new things. She also liked the Schneider family a lot.

Feeling a soft, furry body rubbing against her legs, Lizzy reached down and stroked Marmalade. "Are you hungry, sweetheart?"

She looked up at Lizzy and purred.

"Go ahead and eat. Then we'll go upstairs and make sure you have a safe spot while Harvey's here."

Once Marmalade was settled upstairs, Lizzy texted Jason, and he returned with the dogs. Lizzy went upstairs to get ready for church while he interviewed Mrs. Fickle over breakfast.

"Lizzy," Jason called up the stairs. "We're heading over to check out Mrs. Fickle's house. I'll see you at church."

On the phone with Holly, Lizzy sorted through the clothes hanging in her closet. "Are you going to change after church or just wear the same thing?" she asked.

"I'll just wear the same thing. We won't have a lot of time."

"I have no idea what to wear. I don't have anything pink."

"Just wear what you have, and I'll bring a shirt for you to change into."

"Not red, okay?"

Holly giggled and promised not to bring a red shirt.

Dottie told the volunteers to wear red or pink for Valentine's Day, and although Holly had the same brown eyes and natural hair color as Lizzy, their skin tones made them gravitate to different colors. Holly loved red.

Chapter 13

Disaster

For research purposes, Lizzy paid close attention at church. An usher handed her a bulletin as she and Holly entered the sanctuary and found Thelma Schneider, Holly's mother, sitting with her husband in the third row. The intricate song coming through the organ pipes sounded grand as it bounced off the stone walls. *Maybe I should take piano lessons.*

Lizzy rubbed at the goose bumps on her arms. They had about subsided when Jason slid next to her in the pew. His arm brushed hers, and they popped up again and she shivered.

"Are you cold?" he asked.

"No, I'm fine. I like this music."

"Me too. I'm glad you came."

She stared straight ahead but glanced at him from the corner of her eye. If she hadn't sworn off men after her last toxic relationship… but she had. *There's no way I'm going through that again.* She shook her head.

"What?"

"Nothing. I was just realizing how little I know about church."

As the prelude ended, Pastor Turnbull strode slowly to the front, wearing a white-and-green robe. When he stood at the lectern, he said some opening words, then invited the congregation to recite prayers from the bulletin.

Although she learned some new vocabulary, Lizzy realized one visit was not going to be sufficient. The biblical readings were completely foreign, but she enjoyed the music and the sermon. Pastor Turnbull broke down one of the readings and applied it to everyday life. He spoke of his wife's accident in particular and about turning challenges into opportunities.

The nine o'clock service ended at ten, so they had to hurry. Mrs. Fickle had already taken Mavis with her to greet the other volunteers and offered them tea when they arrived.

Dottie clapped her hands to gain everyone's attention.

"Due to yesterday's mishaps, today we'll be adding arrival and departure times to the guest book. Also, I'd like Lizzy and Mavis to man the table in the sewing room. Coral, you take the kitchen, and I'll monitor the route. Rice, you can start in the prize room. Christine is still absent. Any questions?"

They all shook their heads. Lizzy glanced at their varied expressions and felt a frisson of anxiety. *Please let everything go right today. We should have one smooth day.*

"Go ahead and get some snacks or use the restroom, then take your places. We'll open in thirty minutes," Dottie said. "Lizzy, could I have a word?"

The group disbanded and Lizzy approached Dottie. "Is everything okay?"

"I'm a little worried about yesterday. Sage told me about the break-in last night, and she's worried too. I want to keep a close eye on our guests today; that's why I changed a few of the assignments."

"Good idea. Jason brought Mrs. Fickle over here earlier to see if she noticed anything missing. Did she say?"

"She didn't notice anything, but she's sure it was her cousin. She doesn't want him in the house, so I've asked Holly and Dave to intervene if he shows up again." Suddenly she smiled. "Today everything is going to run perfectly. Go get some snacks and take them upstairs with you. It'll be go time before we know it."

Feeling as if the sun had burst from the clouds, Lizzy smiled back. "Right. Come on, Mavis. There are no snacks like Dottie's snacks." Mavis pranced behind her as she made her way into the kitchen. Sure enough, she found mini quiches, pigs in blankets, homemade chicken nuggets, and appetizer trays from Dave's diner. Someone had even baked heart-shaped sugar cookies.

She piled her plate high and didn't need to call Mavis twice.

Upstairs, Lizzy set her plate on the sewing table and changed into the frilly pink shirt Holly brought for her. *Ugh. I look like a birthday cake.* She checked her phone. Eleven o'clock on the dot. *Mrs. Fickle should be opening the door. The first guests will probably take about ten minutes. Is Rice already upstairs?* Picking up a mini quiche, she took a bite, spraying crumbs everywhere.

Mavis said, "Roherer," and thumped her tail on the floor.

"I know, Mavis. Hold on a sec. These are kind of messy."

Rice rushed by and opened the unmarked door to the attic. The door didn't latch, so Lizzy rose to push it closed. Mavis was quicker though. She hopped up the stairs behind Rice and stood barking on the landing. Rice opened the secret door, her eyes widening as Mavis ran past her and around the bar.

"What on earth?"

Lizzy caught up, following the little dog's frantic barking. As she rounded the end of the bar, she saw the halo of Christine's long blonde hair framing her purple face. Lizzy noted dried red residue in the broken glass that lay on the floor near Christine's outstretched fingers and several footprints in the same color.

Mavis began to howl.

"Go stop the guests from coming up here. I'll call for help." Lizzy dialed Jason's number, but Rice didn't move.

When Jason answered, Lizzy said, "We need help. Mavis found Christine, and she's dead. I think it might be murder." She told him where she was and disconnected.

"Why are you still here?" she asked Rice.

"I don't want you to mess up the scene. Why don't you go?"

Lizzy stared at her, flabbergasted. "Are you kidding me?"

Rice stared back.

Dialing Dottie, Lizzy said, "Stop the guests from coming upstairs. We've found Christine." She was too late. Several couples burst into the room.

"Please return downstairs and wait," Rice said woodenly.

Legs stiff and hackles raised, Mavis stood next to the body as if guarding it. Lizzy knelt on the floor at the opposite end of the bar and called her quietly. Mavis' growl reminded Lizzy of the previous night, and she looked at the footprints more carefully. *Holly? No, that's impossible. I need to talk to her.*

Lizzy's feet went numb as she knelt, but she felt unable to move. The last time she saw Christine, she had been arrogant and confrontational, so full of life. Death had marred her beauty, but Lizzy could still picture her as she was. Thinking back over the events of the day before, she wondered.

"You didn't even like her, did you?" Rice asked.

Lizzy had forgotten she was there. "Neither did you, but that doesn't mean she deserved to die."

The door opened, and though Lizzy couldn't see him from where she knelt, she felt Jason's presence as he strode in. "Where's the body?"

"Over here behind the bar," Lizzy said. Her voice quavered. "Watch out for the footprints."

Jason glanced at Rice standing stiffly with her arms crossed and wished for what seemed like the thousandth time that he hadn't had to relieve her of duty. He observed the footprints Lizzy had mentioned and carefully made his way around the bar.

She was still kneeling just around the corner, and when she looked at him over her shoulder, his heart ached. She looked much as she had when she found Ethel Crocker, but he had grown to understand her a little better.

He held out his hand to help her up, and she winced when she got to her feet. "Can you tell me what happened?"

"M-mavis." Lizzy pointed, and he saw belatedly that Mavis stood over Christine like an ancient sentinel.

"Has she touched the body?"

"No. She just stood there and howled."

Jason ran his finger around his dry lips and thought about that, vaguely wishing he knew an animal behaviorist. "Is that strange?"

"I don't know. She was unconscious when I found Mrs. Crocker."

He turned and looked at Rice. Her lips were flattened into a thin line, and her eyes narrowed. "Are you angry about something?"

"Homicide does that to me."

Deciding to let it go, he asked, "You two were together when you found the body?"

"Yes."

"Can I get Mavis? I didn't want to get near the body before you got here."

"Let's wait for the doc. Why don't you two go stand by the door, and I'll start taking photos." He wanted to comfort Lizzy. The urge to hug her was strong. But he could almost feel the waves of hostility emanating from Rice and didn't want to exacerbate the situation. *Maybe her dismissal affected her a lot more than she let on. Or is it something else? Does she dislike Lizzy?*

He taped off each footprint and took pictures with a small ruler while keeping an eye on Mavis.

He heard the secret door slide open. Heavy breathing and footsteps followed. "Is that you, Doc?"

"Yes, and Barker. Where are you?"

Jason stood. "Over here. Watch the floor."

Steve walked around the bar to Jason and stared at Mavis. "What's the dog doing with the body?"

"She got there first, and I didn't want to disturb anything until you arrived."

"She looks like she might put up a fight. Let's see what we can ascertain before we deal with her. Start with photos."

They didn't get far because when either of them approached the body, Mavis growled.

"Lizzy," Steve said, "Can you try to move your dog without disturbing the body?"

"Sure, Doc. I'm sorry." She carefully approached Mavis and, without pausing, grabbed her around the middle and stepped away. Mavis whined and squirmed, short tufts of fur floating through the air. "I'm almost certain she didn't touch the body, although she might be contaminating the scene with dog hair." She scrunched her nose, and Jason chuckled.

"It's highly unlikely her hair will confuse the cause of death. Thanks for your help," Steve said.

"Go on downstairs now, and please don't discuss what you've seen. I'll be down to interview you both when we're done here," Jason added.

Chapter 14

Aftermath

Two thoughts ran through Lizzy's mind as she descended the stairs. The first was that she should get Mavis home. Then again, perhaps Mavis was better off with her. *I should ask Holly. I also need to talk to her about last night.* That was the second thought. *But Jason told us not to talk to anybody about the murder.*

Doc Steve hadn't said it was murder, but Lizzy had done enough research on poisons to recognize the symptoms.

It was definitely murder.

Guests and volunteers continued to mill around downstairs, chatting and munching on hors d'oeuvres from the kitchen. In the sitting area, Holly was next to Dottie on the sofa, holding her hand. They both looked up at Lizzy when she entered with Mavis, Dottie with a worried frown and Holly with wide, anxious eyes.

Lizzy shook her head. "I'm not supposed to talk about it yet."

"Is she dead?" Dottie asked.

"Please don't make me break my promise. They'll be down to talk to everyone soon."

Dottie leaned back and closed her eyes. "I guess we're done here. I've never had such a miserable event. One thing after another."

Mavis whined and began struggling to get down again, so Lizzy perched on the coffee table and set the little dog next to Dottie on the sofa. She climbed onto her lap and laid her head on Dottie's arm.

"Thank you, Mavis," she said sadly.

The room seemed to shrink when Rice strode in. Hands on her hips, she scowled at Lizzy. "Are you busy spreading rumors already?"

"What is your problem, Rice? I promised I wouldn't, and I'm not."

"Then what are you talking about?"

"The event."

"Same thing, isn't it?"

"I would really appreciate it if everyone could get along for just a few minutes." Dottie sounded tired. "Sometimes I wonder if all our problems are coming from the constant bickering and strained relationships. We've never had trouble like this before."

"None of us would try to shut down the maze," Holly said. "We've worked so hard on it."

"I hope you're right."

Rising from his examination, Steve said, "We'll need an official autopsy, but I can safely say that she was poisoned with some type of cyanide. The time of death was approximately twelve to twenty-four hours ago."

"That's pretty broad."

"I'd lean closer to the middle, but like I said, an autopsy will provide a lot more information. You can also ask the volunteers when they last saw her. That will narrow it down." He closed his bag. "Is the ambulance here?"

"Yes, the EMTs are waiting in the sewing room."

"I'll ride with them to the hospital."

"Thanks, Doc. Let me know when you have more."

Steve left the room, and Jason glanced at Barker. "We've got a lot of evidence."

"Almost too much, don't you think? Why would the killer mix up such a huge batch of cocktails?"

"Maybe it's not all the same."

"We'll have to have it all tested, but even if it's not..." Barker shook his head. "There're puddles of it. Did the perp want to leave footprints? And fingerprints? Some areas have all kinds of prints, but others, like the glass, only have two sets.

"It had to be premeditated. Was the killer really careless or just stupid?"

"Or maybe they thought they were being clever," Jason said. "Gather up everything you've collected, and let's start our initial interviews."

The doctor reentered with the EMTs and was directing them when Jason and Barker left the room. On their way downstairs, Jason said, "She wasn't killed today, so we should concentrate on who was where when they last saw her yesterday. First let's make sure all of the guests have left."

Barker nodded. "I'll start in the kitchen."

They systematically worked their way through the first floor, escorting the guests to the door and sending the volunteers to the sitting room. When they entered the room, Jason surveyed eight individuals, all of whom he knew on a personal level. He didn't want to divulge the cause of death unless absolutely necessary and was considering how to address the group when Dottie spoke up.

"What happened to Christine? Lizzy phoned me to keep the guests downstairs before you came."

"I'm afraid Christine is dead. Doc Steve has taken her to the hospital."

Varying degrees of shock adorned the volunteers' faces, and they murmured among themselves.

"How did she die?" Dave asked.

"I can't divulge that information at the moment. What I would like from each of you is a statement about when you last saw her, who you were with, and what you were doing. That will help us narrow the time of death. Barker will stay here and take everyone's fingerprints while I speak to each of you in the kitchen."

"You don't think one of us killed her, do you?" Holly asked.

"No, I just want a clear picture of where everyone was when she was last seen."

"Lizzy, why don't we start with you so you can take Mavis home?"

She rose quietly and followed him to the kitchen, taking a chair at the table.

"Have you had anything to eat?"

She glanced at the clock. "I had something before I went upstairs."

"Do you remember when you last saw Christine?"

"Yesterday. I was angry with her because she always seemed to be causing trouble." Lizzy looked down.

"Where did you see her?"

"She was in the sewing room, rubbing Coral's back, when Stacy and I went in around one o'clock. You know how jealous Stacy is. I could see from Christine's face that she was playing a game, and I told her to go upstairs, or she'd be replaced. I went with her and told her I'd be back with Dottie."

"What did Stacy do?"

"When I got back, Coral said she'd left. Holly told me she quit and left the house."

"And you never saw Christine again?"

"No. When I went downstairs, that's when the 'rabid dog' thing started, and when I went back up, around two, she wasn't there. Or maybe she was." Lizzy's eyes went wide. "I sent Rice up to cover for her, and then Holly took over. I thought she must have left."

"Do you know who's had arguments with her since she joined the group?"

"Who hasn't?"

"Okay. Thank you. Send Holly in, and you can take Mavis home." He watched her go, wishing he could offer her some type of comfort but needing to remain professional.

Holly was the most difficult, because she didn't understand how he could treat her as a witness. As usual, his sister's face was easy to read when she entered the room. Her reaction to Christine's death caught him off guard. Stiff shoulders, clenched fists, and a furrowed brow gave him pause. "You and Christine were old friends, right?"

"A very long time ago. I don't think she's the same person."

"Did you like her?"

Looking down at her hands, she unclenched them. "I didn't get to talk to her, but she was gossiping about me."

"What's worrying you?"

Her eyes were wide when her head jerked up to stare at him.

"I know you."

"I guess—it's all the other stuff. You sounded like you think one of us killed her. But there was a lot going on yesterday. I even saw Madeline with Mrs. Fickle's cousin."

"How do you know him?"

"I saw him with Mr. Fickle at the Christmas party."

"We'll be thorough. Right now, I'm just trying to narrow down the time of death."

Holly nodded.

"Can you remember the last time you saw her?"

With a pink face and downturned eyes, she said, "We had an argument on Friday, so Lizzy swapped our shifts."

Chapter 15

Secrets

Lizzy made a fire when she got home and put Mavis in her bed. Exhausted from her morning, the little dog burrowed under her blanket and fell asleep.

Lizzy started a pot of coffee and paced back and forth from the kitchen to the front window. When she saw Holly round the corner, she glanced at Mavis, who showed no reaction other than a thump of her tail.

Lizzy opened the door and threw her arms around Holly before she could knock. "Thank goodness you're here."

"What happened?"

"I need to talk to you. Want some coffee?"

"Sure." Holly followed her into the kitchen and sat at the table.

Lizzy poured two cups of coffee and sat with her. "Tell me about your socks."

"Huh?"

"Yesterday Mavis sniffed your feet and howled, remember?"

"That was really weird."

"It's not as weird as you think. What did you step in?"

The round shape of Holly's mouth and eyes would have been comical if not for the seriousness of the question. Lizzy focused on the present, trying mightily not to imagine the scene encroaching into her head.

"How did you know I stepped in something?"

"Please just tell me."

"I don't know what it was; something wet. I was going to go behind the bar to see if I could find a bottle of water, but I took a few steps and felt like my socks were sticking to the floor, so I took them off until they dried."

"You didn't go behind the bar?"

"No. Is that where she was?"

"Where are the socks now?"

Her voice rising, Holly asked, "Are you telling me she was lying dead in that room the whole time I was there?"

Sensing her impending hysteria, Lizzy took her hand and spoke quietly. "I think so. Where are the socks?"

"They're soaking in the bathroom sink. What was it? Blood?" She pulled her hand from Lizzy's and leaned away from her.

Lizzy observed the visible rise and fall of Holly's chest. "Should I get you a paper bag?"

White hands clenched the edge of the table as Holly struggled to slow her breathing. "I didn't kill her. I swear."

"I know that. Jason will know that too. But he might have to arrest you if he's given what looks like solid evidence. That could slow down the investigation."

"You think we should keep it a secret?"

"Not a secret exactly. Maybe just not mention it unless he asks."

They stared at each other across the table.

"I'm really bad at keeping secrets from him."

"I know."

Belatedly released from her room upstairs, Marmalade promptly made herself comfortable in Mavis' bed, gradually expanding until Mavis got up and moved to the other.

"Fascinating," Holly said.

Lizzy thought so too. Her stomach growled, and she glanced at the clock. "Are you getting hungry?"

"I am. A little."

Mavis ran to the door, barking, and the bell rang.

"I guess she's gotten her second wind. Who is it, puppy?"

Lizzy opened the door to find Mrs. Fickle and Madeline Prichard, who was laden down with food from the event. "Good timing. We were just talking about food."

Holly gave a wave from the hall.

Kicking off her boots and shoving the food she was carrying at Lizzy, Madeline exclaimed, "Cleo! There you are." She ran for the cat and fell to her knees, arms extended.

Lizzy gaped as Marmalade meowed at her and jumped into her arms, purring and rubbing against her. She could see their bond as clearly as she saw Marmalade's disinterest on her previous visit.

Madeline stood and carried her cat to the sofa, where she cried and hugged her fiercely. "I thought you were lost."

"I'm so confused. Last time you came to see her, she acted like she didn't know you. This time I can see she loves you. Why?"

"I didn't even know she was here."

"You came with Rice."

"Who?"

"Pearl Rice. She works at the diner."

"Christine's friend. I've never spoken to her."

Concerned about her guest's sanity, Lizzy said, "You came to the committee meeting with her when your husband fell through the roof."

"I don't mean to be rude, but you and I have never met."

She was adamant.

"But…"

"Oh no. No. That can't be. Did she look exactly like me?" Madeline hugged Marmalade too tightly, and the cat hopped off her lap.

Observing her, Lizzy noticed some minute differences in her appearance. "Not exactly, I guess, but almost. No gray in her hair, slightly narrower eyebrows, extremely thin."

"I have a twin sister. I haven't seen her for years, ever since she tried to steal Nap from me."

"How long have you had Marma—Cleo?"

"Years. Since she was a kitten."

"So, your sister met her before?"

"Yes, but she was mean to her. Cleo doesn't like her. Why is she in Harperstown?"

"You would know better than I would." Lizzy shrugged. "Are you acquainted with Mrs. Fickle's cousin Lucian?"

"I've met him. He and Nap did business before we moved here. To tell you the truth, I was glad to get away from him. No offense, Sage, but he's kind of scary."

"None taken, dear. I don't like him either."

"Yesterday I saw you, or your sister maybe, enter the maze with him," Holly said.

"Not me, I can assure you."

"How did you run into Mrs. Fickle this afternoon?"

"I was outside calling my cat, and she invited me over. She didn't tell me Cleo was here."

"I know her as Marmalade." Mrs. Fickle smiled. "Such a sweet kitty. Shall we eat?"

"Let's just lay everything out on the coffee table. I'll get some plates. Watch Mavis." Lizzy set down the food Madeline had handed her and sauntered to the kitchen, calling, "Mavis. are you ready for dinner?"

A quandary. Mavis barked twice and wagged her tail. She ran a couple of steps toward Lizzy, then back to the coffee table. Back and forth. When Marmalade disappeared into the kitchen though, Mavis sprinted behind her. Candy meowed at Holly and jumped down from her lap, running after the other two pets. Lizzy fed all three animals, looking up to see Madeline standing in the archway.

"You've taken very good care of her."

"I've never had a cat before, but I would gladly keep her. She's so sweet."

"I hope you'll let me have her back. She's the only great thing in my life, and I've been heartbroken without her."

"Of course. I never meant to keep her. I was just worried about her after the accident, and I didn't know where you'd gone. Then your sister asked me to take care of her while she was staying in the hotel."

"I really hate her. She's so manipulative."

"We'll find you a ride after dinner. I have quite a few cat things upstairs."

Madeline hugged Lizzy and smiled. Mrs. Fickle stuck her head in the kitchen and said, "Where are those plates?"

Lizzy placed the cat bowls on the counter, rescuing the leftovers from Mavis, then led the way into the living area. Marmalade curled up next to Madeline, and Mavis danced around the coffee table, speaking her own language and practicing her ESP. Candy climbed up Holly's pant leg.

<hr>

After dinner, Holly called Barker and asked him to give Madeline and Marmalade a ride while Lizzy took them upstairs. "The only thing I don't have is a cat carrier," Lizzy said. "I can lend you Mavis', but I'd like to have it back."

Madeline looked around the room in awe. "You got her so much stuff. Can I pay you back?"

"No, that's okay. I enjoyed having her. I was really confused when she was almost hostile toward your sister but so snuggly with me. It didn't make sense."

"That would have been strange if it was me."

"I have one more question if you don't mind. When your sister..."

"Serena," Madeline said.

"When Serena was at the committee meeting, she attacked Christine, calling her a homewrecker. She insinuated your husband had an affair with her."

Madeline shook her head. "I can assure you he didn't, but Christine is known for making passes at men in relationships.

"She might have interfered in one of Serena's relationships. I haven't spoken to her in years, so I don't know if she's married or anything."

"Thanks. Let's get this stuff downstairs." Stopping mid-stride, Lizzy asked, "Does your husband know Serena?"

"No. I…" Madeline's shoulders slumped, and she hung her head. "Serena always wanted whatever I had and usually got it. She took my clothes, my friends, and even tried to take Cleo. So when I caught her trying to seduce my husband, I snapped. I finally stood up for myself and told her I didn't want to see her again. I should have told him, but—I'm ashamed to even say it—I was afraid. I thought he would choose her instead of me."

"It's none of my business, but I think you should tell him."

"But why? After all these years."

Lizzy shook her head, unable to explain her unease. "I don't know why she's here, but if he doesn't know she exists, it makes him vulnerable, doesn't it?"

"Maybe. I'll think about it."

They carried some of the cat supplies downstairs. Barker was standing near the door with Holly.

"Could you help carry the sandbox down?" Lizzy asked.

"You 'betcha."

She smiled at his use of local slang, remembering Jason's face when she had tried it out as a joke.

"I'm going to ride along with them," Holly said. "I'll see you tomorrow."

"I think I'll head for bed." Mrs. Fickle, who'd been quietly sitting in Lizzy's recliner, stood and covered her yawn with her thin hand. "I don't know why I feel so tired."

"We had a lot going on today. Go ahead and get some rest."

Madeline carried Cleo to Barker's cruiser while Lizzy and Holly helped him carry the cat supplies. *I'll never get used to calling her Cleo. I like Marmalade much better.* Lizzy waved as they pulled away from the curb.

Chapter 16

Evidence

Eyes bleary and head pounding, Jason leaned back in the chair behind his desk and stared at the incident board. Harvey, lying by his feet, whined softly. Prior trauma had required early retirement for the somewhat unpredictable German shepherd. He was highly trained and an excellent partner but didn't do well with crowds and had identifiable triggers, one of which was the presence of a handgun.

"We should go visit Mavis." Jason's greatest desire at that moment was to talk to Lizzy. He knew she could help him unravel the evidence, but her friendship with Holly would pose a problem. It was a problem for him too. He had never ignored evidence based on his personal feelings, but he was torn. *I wonder if I should call in the state police.* He shook his head. *They would throw the book at her. I have to keep digging.*

"Come on, Harvey. It's time for a field trip." Jason stood and attached Harvey's leash to his harness, stopping outside for a potty break before opening his cruiser's passenger door for him. Harvey was besotted with Mavis, and when he saw where they were headed, Jason thought his exuberance might cause an accident. "Harvey, sit. You're much too big to be doing that."

Ignoring him, Harvey whined and jumped against the window. Jason pressed harder on the accelerator pedal. They managed the short drive without incident. When Jason pulled up at the curb and opened the passenger door, Harvey raced by him before he could grab his leash. Mavis' barking began before they reached the porch, and Lizzy opened the front door. She stepped out of Harvey's way and laughed as he got down on the floor and wiggled at the sight of Mavis.

They sniffed each other, barking and tearing around the house in a game of tag.

She's so beautiful. I wish I could… no, that would ruin everything. Jason stuffed his feelings out of sight and smiled at her.

"Sorry! Come on in. Those two are so cute."

Removing his boots, Jason followed her into the living area, where she invited him to sit by the fire.

"I suppose it's too late for coffee. Tea maybe?"

"No, I'm good."

"Are you making any progress?"

"Yes and no." He gazed at her, trying to make up his mind. "There's so much evidence, but it doesn't make sense. We still have a lot of digging to do."

"You're exhausted. Scooch around a little, and I'll rub your shoulders."

He did as he was told because his head was still pounding, and his shoulders were up around his ears. At the same time, he was aware that she was withholding the questions she would normally ask. She massaged his head, neck, and shoulders, magically relaxing his muscles one at a time.

⸺ ⋅⋅◦⟨⟩◦⋅⋅ ⸺

Lizzy could see how tired Jason was. He had those pinchy lines between his brows, the ones he got when his head hurt. She assumed that the evidence he mentioned had to do with Holly. Wanting to avoid lying to him, she aimed for distraction instead. Her heart fluttered and her hands trembled when she ran her fingers over the back of his head.

Concentrate, she told herself, feeling carefully for the tightness of his stress. She could feel him begin to relax as she worked her way down to his neck and shoulders, then lowered him gently onto the sofa when he drifted off to sleep.

Looking down at his peaceful face, she ran her slim hands down his muscular arms and rested them on his wide chest.

Finally, she stood and went upstairs to get the blanket he used when he stayed over. She covered him and dimmed the lights, saying good night to the dogs and retiring to her room. Unsure if she should risk waking Mrs. Fickle to let her know they had company, she decided not to disturb her.

Strange dreams once again plagued her as they had since Christine's death. Sometime during the night she woke, heart racing after yet another dream, and was comforted by Mavis' warm body curled up next to her own. She tried to remember the dream but could only recall the end. Two neighbor boys stood over Christine's body, pelting her with gifts from the prize table. *Bizarre*, she thought as she drifted back to sleep.

When she next opened her eyes, Mrs. Fickle was standing in her doorway.

"Do you sleep with that braid?" Lizzy asked.

"No, dear, but it's the first thing I do in the morning. Are you aware that you have an extra dog?"

"Oh. Yes. Sorry. You remember Harvey, Jason's dog. I hope he didn't frighten you. I gather he's a little unpredictable."

"He hasn't paid any attention to me. He and Mavis are sleeping in front of the fire."

"Sounds about right. I'll get up now and make you some break-fast."

"Or I can make it. You don't have to wait on me."

"No problem at all. I'll be down in a minute." Lizzy threw off her covers and rolled out of bed, wondering what the day would bring.

Jason woke to Mavis' unique communication skills. "Ahrooerer," she said. Harvey, on the other hand, stuck his wet nose in his ear then licked his cheek.

"Ugh." He sat up and rubbed his eyes. "You guys are obnoxious."

Mavis barked twice and ran to the door.

Throwing on his coat and boots, Jason opened the front door for them. He didn't have to leave the porch, because they completed their business in record time and returned immediately. Jason looked at his watch and decided there was no sense going back to bed.

Unable to even think until he fed Lizzy's little beast, he gave Mavis and Harvey breakfast and started a pot of coffee. He sat at the kitchen table and thought back to the night before. The lingering feel of Lizzy's soothing fingers on the back of his head made his skin tingle. He smiled to himself and murmured, "I always knew you were magic." The coffee pot made a final gurgle, and he frowned. *How on earth did I fall asleep?* Not only that; it was the best sleep he'd had in ages. *Magic.*

The dogs looked so cozy by the fire that he decided to let Harvey stay. That would give him a chance to return; he still wanted to talk to Lizzy about the evidence. *I do, right? Maybe I shouldn't. Her lack of curiosity last night was odd. Did I look that knackered? I'll try again this evening.* Letting himself out, he returned home to get ready for work.

Barker beat him to the station and was standing in front of the incident board when he arrived. He wore a flat expression when he turned. "Do you think Holly could have murdered Christine?"

"Sit down a minute." Jason moved around his desk and sat, waiting for Barker to join him. "Do you remember when I arrested Lizzy?"

"I do, but you'd just met her. We're talking about someone you've known your entire life."

"I am 99.9 percent sure Holly could never kill anyone, especially someone she hasn't seen for ten years."

"Then why—"

"You know as well as I do that we can't just ignore evidence because we don't agree with it. We have to find an explanation for it."

"Then we'd better get busy because I have no intention of arresting Holly—no matter what."

"My mom would have my head."

They stared at each other in silence for a moment, and then Jason said, "There's something we're missing. The first thing we have to figure out is how Holly's prints got on that glass."

"And the bottle. Has the doc sent the autopsy report?"

"Let me check."

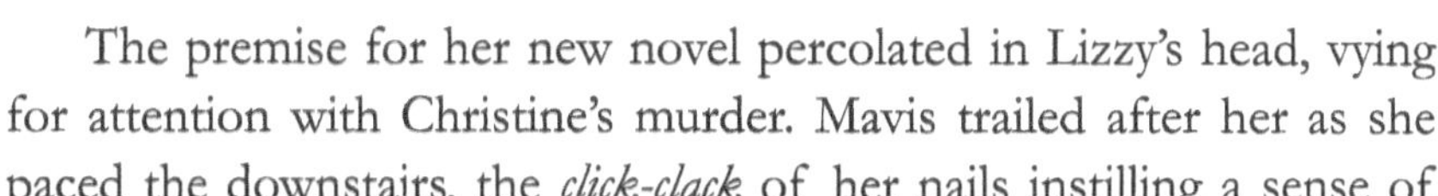

The premise for her new novel percolated in Lizzy's head, vying for attention with Christine's murder. Mavis trailed after her as she paced the downstairs, the *click-clack* of her nails instilling a sense of urgency, like a ticking time bomb.

The metaphorical bomb exploded with the sound of the doorbell. Lizzy stood frozen as Mavis ran to the door, barking, joined by Harvey in a jarring cacophony. Initially annoyed, she decided that perhaps the interruption would give her some respite from her own thoughts.

Mrs. Fickle had gone to visit Holly's mother, Thelma, and Holly was working. Curious, Lizzy opened the front door and gazed at her guest in surprise.

Mrs. Turnbull stood with a cane, one foot and ankle encased in a plastic-covered surgical boot. Without her sizeable husband by her side, she wasn't as tiny as Lizzy had first imagined. Several inches shorter than Lizzy's five foot ten, and a healthy weight, she exuded internal strength and empathy. The almost-tangible power emanating from her produced in Lizzy an immediate need to write. She struggled to remain in the present. Her guest was injured after all. "Please come in. Wasn't it dangerous to walk on the ice?"

"They put traction on my boot." Mrs. Turnbull smiled. "I can see you have something on your mind. Do you need to excuse yourself for a moment?"

"Yes. Please make yourself at home. I'll be right back." Relieved, Lizzy raced to her desk and scribbled in her notebook. She didn't understand, but she was fascinated.

Returning to the living area, she found Mavis on her guest's lap and Harvey sitting on the floor in front of her with his head resting on her knee. Lizzy apologized and asked Mrs. Turnbull if she'd like something to eat or drink.

"Please call me Penelope. I'd love some coffee if you have some made, but I really just wanted to talk to you."

Lizzy was drawn to Penelope like a surfer to the sea. She went to get coffee and returned with a tray, surprised Mavis didn't follow her to the kitchen.

When they were settled, Penelope said, "I know you and Jason are close, and I wanted to ask you if I should tell him about something I noticed before my accident."

Lizzy leaned forward.

"There's always some danger," Penelope began slowly, measuring her words. "Danger of inadvertently spreading misinformation." Her kind face was suddenly serious, her silver eyes studying Lizzy through thick, black-framed glasses. "You don't gossip much, I think."

"I listen to gossip because I'm curious, but you're right; I don't often repeat what I hear."

"Well then, here's my dilemma. Before Marshall and I entered the secret passage, I noticed some local teens running through the rooms, shoving each other, and laughing. I didn't give it much thought until later when I realized they had run from the coat room and ahead of us into the library."

"Did you recognize them?"

Penelope nodded.

"Do they have a history of causing trouble?"

"A little, but I think it might be more than that this time."

"You should talk to Jason even if it amounts to nothing. So many things happened on Saturday; it's difficult to figure out which are connected."

"Thank you. I'll speak with him. This coffee is delicious, by the way."

"I buy it online." Lizzy paused. "I don't mean to pry, but do you need any help with the medical bills?"

"The Lord always provides."

To Lizzy that meant yes. She added a call to the hospital to her to-do list. "One more thing. If someone who knew nothing about religion or church wanted to learn, where would they start?"

Penelope smiled. "Why don't you make an appointment with my husband? He can explain the basics and point you in the right direction."

"How did you know it was me?"

"Just a hunch." She set her cup on the coffee table and rose with the help of her cane. "Marshall is here to pick me up. Thank you for your hospitality."

Lizzy watched from the porch as Pastor Turnbull jogged up the front walk and solicitously helped his wife to the car. Then she hurried to her desk and opened her laptop.

Chapter 17

Sorting the Chaff from the Wheat

When their interview was complete, Jason stood and thanked the Turnbulls for coming in.

"Lizzy told me I should talk to you. You won't take action unless it's absolutely necessary, will you?" Penelope asked.

"I'll verify what I can before I speak with the families."

After they left, Jason sat at his desk and scowled at the incident board. Lizzy. She was always in the middle of everything. Deciding he would confront her after his shift, he studied his notes from the day before. He pressed his intercom and summoned Barker.

When Barker entered, Jason handed him Penelope's statement and waited.

"I'd like to verify the kids' movements before we speak to their families."

Barker nodded his understanding. "Who's first?"

"Let's pay Dottie a visit, then Holly and Coral, I think."

"Let's visit Holly last. I'm taking her to supper."

Jason glared at him, but then, with a change of heart, he grinned. "I guess if she has to date someone, you're better than most. At least I'm pretty sure you're not a homicidal maniac like the last one."

Always sensible and good-natured, Barker grinned back. "Not so far. Ready to go?"

"Yep." Jason stood.

"Where's Harvey?"

"He's at Lizzy's. I couldn't pry him away from Mavis."

The first thing Barker did once they got in the cruiser was crank up the heat, rewarding them both with a blast of frigid air.

Jason shivered.

113

"It'll probably be warm by the time we get there."

"Sounds about right. Why don't you turn it down for now?" He knew Barker's theory was the higher it was turned up, the faster it would get warm, but it was worse than having the window down.

Jason parked in the no-parking zone in front of the Hummingbird bakery, causing Barker to tut-tut.

"Come on. We won't be long."

The bakery always felt like a warm hug. Soft music, heat from the ovens, and the sweet fragrances of fresh cinnamon rolls and chocolate croissants enveloped them as they entered.

Dottie smiled in welcome. "Hello, officers. I don't often see you here together."

"We'd like to ask you a couple of questions if you aren't too busy," Barker said.

Looking around the nearly empty bakery, she said, "I think we're safe for the moment. Can I get you anything?"

"I'll get something to go when we're finished," Jason said.

"Me too, but maybe I'll have a hot chocolate to warm me up," Barker added.

"Okay. Two hot chocolates. I'm buying." Sitting at the table closest to the counter, Jason wrapped his hands around the warm Styrofoam cup.

"How can I help you?"

"We're looking into the movements of several people who attended the maze on Saturday. Since you were in the hall when things started to go wrong, we thought you might be able to add some details. Think about what you were doing before everyone started running around and screaming."

Dottie's eyes rolled up and to the left, lips pressed together. "Sage handed me the cash box and walked away."

"Imagine looking around after she left. What did you see?"

She shook her head. "People were headed in every direction."

"No one in particular caught your attention?"

"Well, I did notice Ron and Chad running around.

"I was going to ask them to settle down, but then the screaming started, and I got distracted."

"Did you see them again later?"

"I didn't notice. I'm sorry."

Jason thanked her and said they had to be going. He paid for the hot chocolates and his to-go order, which both he and Dottie knew was for Lizzy. Barker's was likely for himself, since Holly's kitchen was always full of her own baking. In fact, if he was Barker, he'd just wait until they got there.

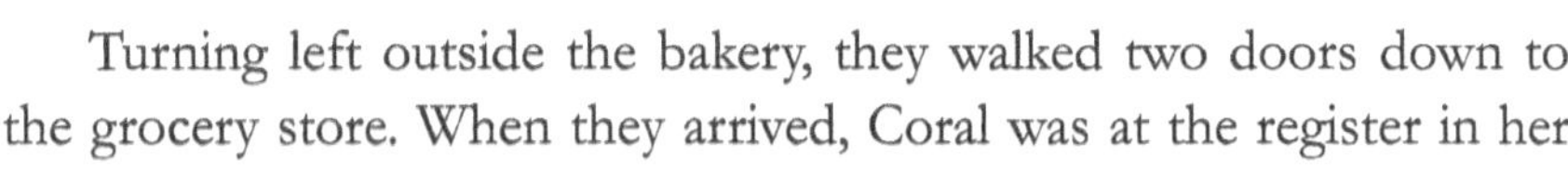

Turning left outside the bakery, they walked two doors down to the grocery store. When they arrived, Coral was at the register in her usual crop top and jeans, chatting happily as she rang up customer purchases.

Jason nodded at Barker, who approached the register and spoke to her. Barker then nodded back and turned to ascend an almost-hidden staircase. The grocery was the most dangerous place to discuss anything private, and Coral was a self-proclaimed disseminator of information. Not her own, perhaps.

Barker waited for Jason on the second-floor landing and knocked before entering the office, where Coral's uncle, the owner, stood before a wall of one-way windows with his hairy hands clasped behind his back. "What brings you here?"

"We need to ask Coral a few questions," Barker said.

"Is she in trouble?"

"No, we just need some additional information."

"Can't it wait until she's off work?"

"No. We need to get this cleared up as soon as possible."

Coral's uncle sighed. "Fine. I'll send 'er up."

"Could you pause the recorder?" Jason asked.

Another sigh. He shuffled over to the file cabinets and pushed a button.

115

After he left, Jason said, "Check it to make sure."

Barker strode to the file cabinets, picked up an old-fashioned tape recorder, and pushed a button. "How did you know?"

"I've known him for a long time."

"My uncle's not too happy about this." Coral tossed her short, teased hair as she entered the office.

"I know, and I'm sorry," Jason said. "We'd just like to ask you what you recall right before Mrs. Turnbull's accident."

"Is she going to sue? I knew it."

"No, nothing like that. Could you hear her husband calling for help when she fell? I mean, how soundproof are those doors?"

"I couldn't hear anything. I wondered why no one was coming through."

"How did you find out?"

"Lizzy came up and told me there was a meeting. Everyone was talking about it when I went downstairs."

"Who were the last people you saw before Lizzy?"

Coral shrugged. "I don't know. I wasn't paying attention. Stacy was so mad, and I'm sure Christine did it on purpose."

"When Lizzy went up to tell you about the meeting, Christine wasn't at her post. Did you see her leave?"

"No. I must have been in a daze. I don't remember seeing any-one. Can I go back to work now?"

"Yes. Thank you for your help."

Coral left the office, and Barker asked, "Why didn't you tell her not to spread it around?"

"Reverse psychology. I figured if I made it sound important, she'd be more likely to talk about it."

"Good thinking."

"Last stop Holly's. I'll move the car in front of Lizzy's."

"You do know the whole town thinks you're having a torrid affair, right?"

"You don't?"

"Nah. If you were, both of you would be a lot more relaxed." Barker let out a noisy guffaw, then looked at Jason's face and went silent.

"Let's go grill my sister."

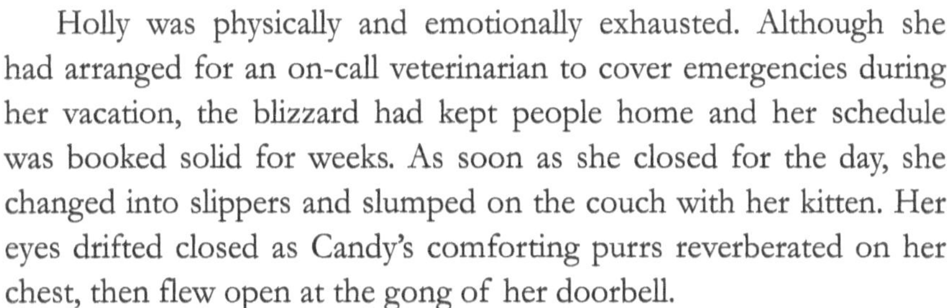

Holly was physically and emotionally exhausted. Although she had arranged for an on-call veterinarian to cover emergencies during her vacation, the blizzard had kept people home and her schedule was booked solid for weeks. As soon as she closed for the day, she changed into slippers and slumped on the couch with her kitten. Her eyes drifted closed as Candy's comforting purrs reverberated on her chest, then flew open at the gong of her doorbell.

She shuffled to the entrance, still carrying Candy, and opened the door. "You're early, aren't you?" She felt aflutter at the sight of Barker, then forced herself to calm down when she saw that Jason was with him.

"I am, but you were on our list of interviews, so we saved you for last. Are you okay?"

"Just really tired. It's been a busy day. Come in."

She stepped aside to let them pass, and as they removed their boots asked, "Should we sit in the living room?"

"Sure. Wherever you're comfortable."

Resuming her seat on the couch, Holly waited. She noticed Jason's unusual silence and wondered if he had discovered her secret.

"Let's start with Saturday morning," he said. "You were in the hall when the guests started screaming and running around, right?"

Holly relaxed slightly. "Yes. A group of people were asking me about the clue in the bathroom."

"Did you notice anything odd before or during that time?"

"Not really. I was about to have a word with a couple of rowdy boys, but then everything kind of happened at once."

"Ron and Chad?"

Holly nodded.

"Can you remember anything else?"

"No, I don't think so."

Jason paused, and she thought he was going to ask her something else, but he stood. "I guess I'll make myself scarce. You two have a nice supper."

"Jason. I have to tell you something."

He sat back down.

"I don't know how to start."

"Start wherever you want. We can always go back."

"I went to Lizzy's house after we closed on Saturday, and when I took my boots off, Mavis sniffed at my feet and started howling. She wouldn't let me pick her up, and she wouldn't eat dinner. Lizzy said she paced and whined all night.

"When I got home and was getting ready for bed, my socks stuck to my feet and I remembered stepping in something sticky, so I put them in the sink with some detergent and left them to soak."

Jason leaned forward and frowned but didn't interrupt.

"Sunday, after you interviewed Lizzy, she asked me to come over when I was done." She glanced at Jason. "She started asking me questions about what I stepped in and when, then asked where my socks were."

"Did she describe the murder scene?"

Shaking her head, Holly said, "She thought it might be better if I didn't know."

"Why didn't you tell me about this right away?"

"Lizzy thought—" She stopped abruptly when she saw his face. "She was thinking of you."

His voice was calm, but his face was thunderous. "How can withholding evidence from a police officer be helping him?"

"She thought if you had to worry about me, it would just distract you. She knew I didn't do it, and she said the best way we could help was to figure out who did." *Oh gosh. I've really put my foot in it.*

"I'm sorry. It made sense at the time. We really were just trying to help."

Jason stood and stuffed his hands in his pockets. He paced to the door and back again. He stopped and stood in front of Holly, looking down at her, and she thought fancifully of an angry, towering tree.

"Perhaps you can tell me how the victim came to be holding a glass with your fingerprints on it."

"A glass?" Holly's heart raced. She was in a lot of trouble. "Are you going to arrest me?"

"Not at the moment, because I still have a lot of questions and I can't see a motive," he said gruffly. "Go have your supper. We'll talk in the morning after I've had a word with your busybody friend." He stomped to the front door and shoved his feet into his boots without looking at Barker or saying goodbye.

Holly watched him go, then glanced at Barker. "Do you still want to have supper with me?"

"Absolutely. Don't worry about Jason. He'll get over it."

"I should have told him."

"Yes. But I understand why you didn't."

"You're pretty awesome." Holly forced a smile.

"I found a wonderful little restaurant in Sioux Falls. Why don't you go ahead and get ready? I'll go get my car and change my clothes. Is an hour enough?"

She nodded and managed to hold back her tears until he left.

Chapter 18

Cold War

In the throes of anger, Jason knew he should wait to confront Lizzy, but he couldn't. She had gone too far. He stomped across the street and pounded on her door. Mavis' barking sounded from inside, followed by breaking glass. He pounded again. "Lizzy?"

She was laughing as she opened the door on her knees, wrapped in two leashes. The dogs bounded around her in opposite directions. Jason almost laughed, but then he remembered he was angry.

"I'm glad you're here." Lizzy looked up at him. "Can you give me a hand?"

He unclipped the leashes from their respective harnesses and took a step back. "We need to talk."

"What is it?" Still busy untangling herself, she hadn't noticed his expression. When she did, she went still. "Has something happened?"

"You could say that. Holly told me about the socks."

"Oh. That's good, I guess?"

"It is good. What's not good is that you encouraged her not to tell me. You deliberately withheld evidence and interfered with a homicide investigation. You've gone too far this time. I could arrest you for this."

She drew her eyebrows together. "It wouldn't be the first time."

"That's not what we're talking about."

"Apparently it is, since you brought it up."

"*You* brought it up."

"Every time I make you mad, you're just going to throw me in jail, right? Not only is that a rotten example of friendship, but I would call it an abuse of power. Why don't you just take your dog and leave? I don't need friends like you."

Standing on her porch with Harvey, Jason's head spun. *What just happened? I was the one with the grievance. How did I end up the bad guy?* He was still upset with her, but he'd lost his chance to express himself. "Come on, Harvey. Let's go home."

⁘⸫⸻⸺⊰⊱⸺⸻⸫⁘

Heart pounding, Lizzy slammed her front door and stalked to the kitchen. She sat at the table and put her head in her hands. Jason was right to be angry. She knew that. But threatening to arrest her again had brought on a visceral reaction. *We're supposed to be friends, aren't we? Why would he say that? Did he arrest Holly? Where is she? If they arrested her, they'll have her phone. Barker wasn't with him. What does that mean?*

She sat thinking until Mavis barked once. "What is it, puppy? You already ate." Mavis barked again and ran for the door.

"Oh no. I'm sorry." Lizzy put their coats on and opened the front door. Mavis ran for the shoveled area where she did her business. Lizzy counted to twenty. "You really had to go."

Back inside, she received a text message from Holly. "R U OK?"

"I should be asking you. What happened? Can I come over?"

"Supper date w/Steve. Valentine's. Told J about socks. So mad. Said something about my fingerprints on a glass. Can I come over when I get back?"

"Yes. Come no matter what time."

"K thx."

Lizzy put her phone down. *Fingerprints? That's even worse. No wonder he was so upset. He would have arrested anyone else. Is someone trying to frame her?* Her stomach rumbled, and she glanced at Mavis. "Want to go to Dave's?"

Mavis barked twice and danced around in a circle. "Okay. Let's get bundled up again. I'll sure be glad when it warms up."

Walking uphill against the frigid wind was miserable, even for just one block. Nose frozen and eyes tearing, Lizzy opened the door to the diner with relief.

Even if she hadn't been hungry, the blast of warm air and din of cheerful voices would have lured her inside. The tantalizing smell of grilled meat reached her as her nose quickly thawed. Rice waved from behind the cash register and grabbed a menu on her way to the door.

"Hi, Lizzy. Where would you like to sit?"

Surveying the busy restaurant, Lizzy asked, "Do you have a small table in a corner somewhere, or should I sit in the bar?"

"Wait just a moment. I have the perfect table for you."

She watched Rice bustle around, removing Mavis' coat as she waited.

When Rice returned, Lizzy asked, "Have you been promoted?"

"I have. When Dave found out I was going to take a second job, he made me the manager."

Lizzy raised her eyebrows. "A second job?"

"Holly didn't tell you? She asked if I'd like to help out in the clinic for a while. I was going to, but Dave said he needed me here."

"Congratulations. That's great."

"Can I get you started with a drink? Something to keep you warm on the way home?"

Lizzy ordered a Long Island iced tea and a burger, even though Rice wasn't her waitress.

"I'll put your order in, but Bob will be your server this evening."

"Thanks. I appreciate it." She caught Rice dropping something from her apron pocket and looked down to see Mavis chomping on whatever it was. "What's she sneaking you, Mavis?"

Mavis ignored her.

As he often did, Dave was making the rounds. He stopped at her table. "How are you this evening?" he asked.

"All is well."

"Where's Holly?"

"She's on a date." Lizzy winked.

"Do tell." He sat on the chair across from her and leaned in.

"I'm not sure it's gossip-worthy yet."

"It's certainly better than the alternative. Who's she out with?"

Lizzy considered any possible downsides to letting him know. She didn't think it was a secret. "Barker."

Dave stroked his black goatee and nodded. "A solid choice. What's Jason think about it? Does he know?" His eyes twinkled.

"I think he's okay with it, but you'd have to ask him."

"Ever the diplomat." He chuckled. "Have you heard anything more about Christine?"

Lizzy shook her head. "No, just that they're interviewing people."

"Do you ever write about true events? Maybe this will end up in your next book."

"No, but I've got some ideas bouncing around in my head."

"I can't wait. I've read them all so far, and I need another."

"I guess I'd better get busy then."

Bob arrived with her burger, so Dave excused himself and left her to her meal.

Mavis, on her best behavior, didn't bark at Dave, but she smelled Lizzy's burger and whined softly.

"You know I'll give you some."

Mavis stared at her intently.

Cutting a piece of meat off the patty, Lizzy placed it on a small plate and set it next to Mavis. Then she cut the burger in half and took a bite. Chewing slowly, she relished the combination of grilled meat, bacon, cheese, and vegetables, wishing only that it was slightly thinner. She smashed it with her fingers so she could get her mouth around it and ended up with ketchup on her cheek and mayonnaise on her chin. Before she could wipe the offending condiments off, she looked up to find Jason staring at her.

Seated in the bar area with two men she hadn't seen before, he turned his head toward one of his companions and said something to make him chuckle. He didn't look at her again.

Lizzy wanted desperately to leave, but she knew from experience that the left-over burger would end up in the trash. She ordered another drink and concentrated on ignoring him. By the time she took her last bite, he was gone.

Glad but deeply unhappy at the same time, she asked for the check.

"The captain already paid for your meal," Bob told her.

Her burger was a lump of lead in her stomach. Her muscles contracted, and she felt sick.

"Are you okay?"

"Yes, fine," she croaked.

Rice arrived at the table with a smirk. "Trouble in paradise?"

"I don't get you, Rice. Sometimes you seem so nice, and sometimes… Sometimes you really don't."

"Gotta keep you on your toes." She grinned. "Can I get you anything else?"

Lizzy just shook her head. She bundled Mavis and left as quickly as she could. When they got home, she forgot Holly was supposed to visit and flopped across her bed fully dressed.

Barker returned to Holly's house to pick her up for their date. He helped her into his Ford pickup and drove the thirty minutes to Sioux Falls in silence. Although they didn't know each other well, Holly was pleased that he didn't seem to require constant conversation. She wanted to ask him about the crime scene but was afraid he'd refuse to discuss it. She was also afraid he suspected her of murder.

Entering Sioux Falls, he glanced at her and asked, "Do you like Asian food?"

"I think so. Maybe. I've only had it a couple of times."

"I don't know how good it is, but I found a buffet with Chinese, Japanese, and American food.

"The reviews are good. And we can try everything."

"That's a great idea." Holly smiled.

He pulled into a nearly full parking lot and walked around to the passenger side of his truck to help her out.

He's such a gentleman, she thought. *It's so far up off the ground.* The little metal step was slick and icy, and when he reached up for her, she felt like a medieval princess alighting from her carriage.

When they entered the noisy restaurant, Holly saw the rows and rows of food and wondered how she would ever choose. "You haven't been here before?"

"No, but I've been wanting to try it out. I hope it's good."

"It smells wonderful. Lizzy would be in seventh heaven."

"Maybe we should invite her and Jason next time."

"If they're still speaking. He was sure mad."

They spent hours in the restaurant, sampling everything until they couldn't eat another bite. Holly thought their conversation could be compared to a buffet as well. They talked about their likes and dislikes, childhoods, families, and past relationships.

When they returned to her house, Barker stayed to watch a movie, and she completely forgot Lizzy was expecting her.

⁕

Impatient as ever, Mavis jumped around the bed like a rabbit. "Roherer." She hopped down her doggy stairs and back, barking twice and nudging Lizzy's arm.

"Augh. Stop it." Lizzy squinted at her alarm clock. "Can't you get up at a normal time?"

Mavis barked again and ran for the door.

Stumbling down the stairs behind her, Lizzy threw on her coat as she opened the door.

Mavis stopped, sniffed a bakery box sitting on the porch, and pounced on it, her barking frenzied.

When Lizzy bent to pick up the package, Mavis barred her teeth and growled. She nipped Lizzy's hand and took off at a run, sprinting down the walkway to the sidewalk and around the corner.

Lizzy stared after her in shock, then she sighed and went back in to put on her boots.

Mrs. Fickle popped her head through the kitchen arch.

"What—"

"Mavis just took off. There's a package on the porch." She left the house and trudged in the direction Mavis went.

"Mavis," she called. "Where are you?"

At the end of the block, Mavis sniffed at the base of a tree. She squatted to do her business, and then she sat and waited.

Lizzy ran her fingers through her already-tousled hair and observed the little dog. Although she used a harness, Mavis had never given her a reason. Her behavior that morning was concerning. "What's wrong with you? Should we go see Holly?"

Mavis barked and wagged her tail.

"You're a weird dog."

When they got home, the package was open on the kitchen table and Mrs. Fickle was lying unconscious on the floor. Mavis stood over her and howled.

"No. Not again."

Lizzy called 911, unlocked the front door, and began CPR. Time slowed. As she had been irreverently taught, Lizzy hummed "Another One Bites the Dust" while she performed chest compressions. "Come on, Mrs. Fickle. Hold on. Help's on the way."

The paramedics burst through the front door and took over, asking what seemed like a million unanswerable questions. They took the box of pastries, including the partial one lying next to Mrs. Fickle's hand, and loaded her into the ambulance.

Lizzy wanted to go with her, but Jason arrived right behind the ambulance and told her to have a seat. The pinched look on his face brooked no argument. "Tell me what happened."

Lizzy told him.

"Who left the box?"

"I don't know. It was from the Hummingbird, so I thought… I don't know what I thought. Mavis didn't give me time to think."

"Stay there." He pulled out his phone. "Do you know anything about a box left on Lizzy's porch?" He listened for a moment. "I need you to close the clinic and come over. Now."

Lizzy breathed deeply. She could feel the heavy thuds in her chest. Mavis had settled down next to her on the sofa, the dog's head on her thigh.

When Holly arrived, Jason instructed her to sit next to Lizzy. "I should have arrested you yesterday; then you'd have an alibi. Because I put family before duty, I've done you more harm than good. Where did those pastries come from?"

"They were sitting on my porch this morning." Tears trickled down Holly's cheeks. "What happened?"

"Mrs. Fickle has been rushed to the hospital. Does she have any food allergies?"

Holly looked at Lizzy. "I don't think so. Does she?"

"Not that I know of. Plus, Mavis…"

"I don't think we can use a dog as a witness," Jason said.

"Maybe not, but her reaction was odd."

"The two of you have placed me in a bad spot. You are not to leave this house. Nettle will stay here with you."

"You'll let us know how Mrs. Fickle's doing?" Holly asked.

"Yes." He went to the front door and sent Nettle in.

Lizzy didn't like Nettle. He was the lazy, arrogant deputy who had falsely arrested her when she first moved to Harperstown. She and Holly sat on the sofa and stared at him.

Chapter 19

Divine Guidance

On his way to the hospital, Jason stopped at the rectory. Pastor Turnbull was waiting for him and invited him into his study. Jason slouched into the visitor's chair, feeling adrift.

"Tell me what's going on."

"I feel like I've lost control."

"Control of what?"

"Everything."

"Why don't you start at the beginning?"

"I'm not sure when it started. At the maze, I guess. I have a murder to investigate and now what looks like attempted murder. My sister is somehow involved, and Lizzy's mad at me."

"Are the murders connected?"

"Most likely, but I don't know of any motive."

"And how is Holly involved?"

"I don't know that either, but all the evidence is pointing at her. It's just a big mess."

"Why is Lizzy angry with you?"

"I was mad at her and said something she misunderstood."

"So your relationship is repairable."

"Possibly. I think maybe I should call in the state police, but I'm afraid."

"Afraid for Holly?"

Jason nodded.

The pastor put his fingertips together and looked over them at Jason. "You're a good policeman and a good judge of character. I think you know you don't have to do everything alone. God and his Holy Spirit are always with you."

Jason hung his head. *Do I believe that? Really believe it, deep down?*

"Let's pray together now, then I want you to try giving up your need for control." At Jason's look, he added, "What do you have to lose?"

"Okay. I'll try."

Pastor Turnbull lowered his head and closed his eyes. "Most gracious Father, please fill your son Jason with your Holy Spirit. Shower him with your infinite wisdom and peace. Let him feel your powerful presence as he grapples with his personal and professional conflicts. Thank you, Father, for never leaving us to do battle alone. In Jesus' name we pray, Amen."

"Amen," Jason said. He opened his eyes and gazed at the pastor. "I feel calm. Perhaps it's psychosomatic."

Pastor Turnbull smiled serenely.

"Thank you. I'll let you know how it turns out." Jason rose and shook hands, then returned to his cruiser and called Barker. "How is she?"

"Still unconscious, but she'll make it. Doc Steve wants to talk to you."

"I'm on my way."

Barker was waiting for Jason when he arrived and led him to Mrs. Fickle's room. Steve looked up from a file he was studying when they entered.

"Hey, Doc. I hear you have news."

"I do, and I don't think you're going to like it."

Jason sat at a little table by the window and waited.

"I have the autopsy results here, and also the lab report on the pastry Mrs. Fickle ate."

"Start with the pastry."

"The pastry was laced with phenobarbital. Luckily, Mrs. Fickle had a severe reaction, because if she'd eaten the entire pastry, she probably would have died."

"Did the lab test all the pastries?"

"Yes. Only two of the four contained phenobarbital."

"So theoretically, someone could have eaten one and been fine, then someone else could have come along and eaten one and died."

Steve slowly gave a single nod.

"Is there any significance in the type of drug used or why only two pastries were poisoned?"

"The drug is a controlled substance used by veterinarians. My best guess? It was stolen from Holly's clinic, and she had a limited supply."

"What would Holly use it for?"

"Pet euthanasia. She probably orders it as she needs it."

Jason thought about that. *How many pets might need to be put down in a year? Not many.* "And a dose that would kill a person would probably be larger than one used for a small animal."

"Possibly. But a miniscule dose can be fatal."

"Now I wish we hadn't started with the pastries. Does Dottie have any idea who purchased them?"

"I asked her, of course. She doesn't remember anyone ordering those four pastries in a box."

"So someone took pains to put items from separate orders together?"

"I really don't know. It's pure speculation at this point."

Taking a deep breath and letting it out slowly, Jason said, "Okay. What about Christine's autopsy?"

The doctor picked up a file and handed it to Jason. "The official time of death was between one thirty and two p.m. on Saturday. The cause of death was acute potassium cyanide poisoning. The details are in the file, but nothing unexpected. Barker told me that the glass and the decanter had only the victim's and Holly's prints on them, but they were at opposite ends of the bar."

"There were a number of heavy glass decanters, weren't there? They were just for show, with water in them."

Standing in the corner with his arms crossed, Barker said, "There was one at the very end of the bar that contained the same drink we found in Christine's glass. The big question is how did it get there?"

"I have an idea," Steve said, "although it's theoretical."

"Let's hear it," Jason said.

"It's possible that Christine picked up the decanter and poured herself a drink. It smelled sweet. Maybe it tasted very good, so she began to pour herself another after she gulped down the first. The poison seized her, and she flung the decanter as she fell. That would account for the puddles of liquid. When Holly stepped in one of the puddles at the end of the bar, she looked down at her feet and possibly saw the decanter on the floor. Being fastidious by nature, she picked it up and placed it on the bar."

"There's no way to prove that."

"True. But you could ask Holly if she saw a decanter lying around or if she picked anything up off the floor and put it on the bar."

Lizzy sat silently with Holly for a long time, then decided to make Nettle work for a change. "Let's go make some lunch."

"You mean you want me to make dinner?" Holly grinned.

"Maybe." Lizzy ignored Holly's correction. "Or you can teach me how to make something yummy if I have the ingredients."

"Let's see what you've got."

Mavis jumped up and tagged along when they headed for the kitchen, barking and wagging her tail.

"She didn't have breakfast this morning. I can't believe she's been so quiet."

"It's only nine, if you can believe that. I guess you missed breakfast too. Should I just make some bacon and eggs?"

A loud growl emanated from Lizzy's stomach. "Yes, please. I'll feed Her Majesty."

By the time they sat down to eat, her stomach was rioting. She ate a few bites, then stopped and glanced at Nettle, standing in the corner. No, she didn't like him. She hadn't asked him to be there. But they had plenty, and she felt guilty eating in front of him.

"Would you like something to eat?" she asked.

"No, but thank you."

She lifted one side of her mouth at Holly and took a big bite of bacon. "You know what we're missing?"

"Coffee," they said in unison.

"Mrs. Fickle made some this morning, but it's cold. Is it okay if I just reheat it?"

"Sure. I'm not picky."

"Cut it out, Mavis," Lizzy said on her way to the coffee pot.

Mavis sat, looking up at the table intently. Nothing moved but a slight twitch of her tail.

"Can I give her a Beggin' Strip?"

"After breakfast. She's already incorrigible."

Holly giggled. "She is persistent."

"I'll have to take her outside, Deputy, unless you'd like to do the honors."

"I'm just here to observe." He crossed his arms.

After they ate, they did the dishes and took Mavis outside. Deputy Nettle stood on the porch. Lizzy tackled Holly, and they rolled around in the snow, laughing until they cried. That led to a snowball fight, Mavis running back and forth trying to catch them.

Dottie pulled up in her pink Jeep and got out with a big grin. "Looks like you ladies are having a good time. What's he doing here?" She jerked a thumb toward Nettle.

"Babysitting," Lizzy said. "Did you hear about Mrs. Fickle?"

"You forget who I'm married to. I heard."

"It happened here."

"I see. Lizzy, I wanted to talk to you. Suppose we can divide and conquer." She nodded toward the porch.

"Hard to say who he might follow."

"We'll work on it. Got any tea?"

"Naturally."

They tromped through the snow to the porch, Mavis bounding after them. "Hello, Nettle," Dottie called with a wave.

"Hello, Ms. Dottie. I don't know if we're supposed to have guests."

"I'm sure it's fine. Call Jason if you're worried about it. I need to use the restroom."

"Go ahead," Lizzy said. "I have to change. I'm soaked. Can you start the tea, Holly?"

"Sure. Then can I borrow something dry to wear?"

"Of course. Be right back."

Nettle stood in the middle of the open-plan first floor and watched them walk in three different directions.

<hr>

Jason let himself into the house without knocking and found Nettle alone, scratching his balding head.

"What's going on?"

"They were out with the dog…"

Clanking from the kitchen had Jason moving in that direction. Nettle trailed him to find Holly making tea.

"Where's Lizzy?"

Holly turned. "Hi, Jason. We got wet outside, so she went to change. I'm next."

He crossed his arms. "What aren't you telling me?"

She gazed at him with wide, innocent eyes but he wasn't fooled. The tips of her ears turned pink.

"Oh hi, Jason." Dottie entered the room.

He narrowed his eyes. "Where's Lizzy?"

"I don't know. I had to use the restroom."

"I'm here. Your turn, Holly. Just use whatever fits. I left out some sweatpants that might work."

"Okay. The tea's ready, Dottie."

"Proper tea?"

"Yes, ma'am. Be back in a sec."

It occurred to Jason that no mere mortal man would be a match for this wily group of females, especially Nettle. He couldn't even blame him.

"What brings you here, Dottie?" he asked.

"Well, if you want to know the truth—"

Jason expected a whopper.

"—I wanted to tell Lizzy something I found out about Saturday's sabotage."

"And you didn't want to tell her in front of Nettle?"

"No."

"Why not?"

"It's rather sensitive."

"And you have relayed your information?"

"Yes. I'll just go now. Steve will be wanting dinner."

"Are you planning on withholding this information as well?" He saw Dottie's look of surprise, but he was focused on Lizzy.

"No, but I think you already know the who, just not the why."

"All right, Dottie. You may go."

She nodded and left.

"I'm not the bad guy, you know," Lizzy said.

"Yes, I know." He looked into her eyes and knew everything would be okay. "You can go now, Nettle. Report to Barker at the hospital."

"Yes, sir."

Nettle left, and Jason held out his arms.

Lizzy walked into his embrace and stayed there until it seemed she was starting to feel uncomfortable. As she stepped back, he took her chin and looked down into her face. "I don't like it when we fight."

"Me neither." She took another step away.

"What's going on?" Holly entered the kitchen and looked from one to the other.

"We've called a ceasefire," Lizzy said. "Want to hear what Dottie had to say?"

"Yes!"

"Several of the older families in this neighborhood were against the mystery maze's real estate angle. They don't want outsiders buying up property and changing things. Their prime example was Mr. Prichard."

"Yeah?" Jason said slowly.

"Apparently they sent their kids to try to shut it down."

"How did Dottie find out?" Jason asked, making Holly giggle.

"It is hard to keep a secret in this town, but Dottie overheard the kids laughing about it in the grocery. She said she hadn't even known about some of the pranks."

"No mention of the murder? Seeing the body or anything?"

"No. I don't think they would have been so gleeful otherwise."

"I'll have to speak with their parents, but at least we're narrowing it down." He looked at Holly. "More bad news for you, I'm afraid. The pastry Mrs. Fickle ate was full of phenobarbital."

Her eyes rolled back, and she collapsed onto the floor.

Lizzy tried to catch her but went down under her dead weight. They both hit the floor, but Lizzy at least cushioned Holly's head from the blow. "Oww," she said.

Jason dropped to his knees. "Are you okay?"

"Yeah."

Holly opened her eyes. "Why are we all down here?"

"You fainted," Jason said.

"I don't faint."

They stared at her.

"What? Oh no. Did you say phenobarbital?"

"Why?" Lizzy asked. "What's the big deal?"

Holly shuddered. "It's commonly used for pet euthanasia."

"You have it at the clinic?"

"Yes. What's going on?"

"It seems to me that someone is trying really hard to frame you," Lizzy said.

"But why?"

"That's the big question, isn't it?"

"Maybe." Jason looked at Lizzy. "But we also have to consider who wanted Christine dead and why the pastries were left on Holly's doorstep. Were they meant for you, or did the person who left them know you would give them away?"

"How would they know that? I didn't have time for breakfast and almost ate one myself."

"Maybe the murderer wants you out of the way so you can't defend yourself," Lizzy said.

"You guys are scaring me."

"One more question, Holly." Jason remembered what he wanted to ask his sister. "On Saturday, when your sock got wet, did you happen to see anything lying around on the floor? Anything you might have picked up?"

She started to shake her head and then stopped. "I completely forgot about that. How did you know?"

"What was it?"

"There was a decanter on the floor. I saw it when I bent down to pull my sock off, so I picked it up and put it on the bar."

Jason was hoping it would be something like that. He blew out a sigh of relief and said, "I have to go. Can you two stick together for the time being?"

"How can we do that?" Lizzy asked. "Holly has to work."

"She's probably safe enough at the clinic, but don't eat or drink anything if you don't know where it came from."

"Can I stay here tonight?" Holly asked Lizzy.

"Of course. We can go get Candy and your overnight bag before it gets too late."

Holly looked at Jason. "Mrs. Fickle's going to recover?"

He nodded. "She was lucky."

"When can we see her?"

"In a day or two, I think."

"I feel so guilty," Lizzy said. "She was staying here because she felt safer. Mavis made sure I didn't touch that box, but… Holly, she howled when we found Mrs. Fickle, just like she howled at your socks."

"And Christine's body," Jason said.

"Do dogs have some way of recognizing poison?"

"I don't think so," Holly said. "But Mavis is unusual."

"We'll give her that. Where is she anyway?" Lizzy swung her head from side to side. "She went upstairs with me earlier, and I'm pretty sure she came back down with me."

"She's usually in here whenever we are."

"Mavis?" Lizzy wandered out of the kitchen and into the living area. The dog bed was empty. "Mavis!"

"Could she have followed Dottie or Nettle outside?" Jason asked.

Rushing past him to the front door, Lizzy flung it open and stared. Mavis sat on the porch with Marmalade. She barked once and thumped her tail, looking extremely proud of herself.

Chapter 20

Where's Madeline?

Observing the two animals, Lizzy asked, "What are you doing here, Marmalade?" She stepped back. "Come on. It's cold out there." Marmalade rubbed against her leg.

"I thought she was staying here," Jason said.

"She was. You said you have to go, but I have another story for you when you come back."

"It's a good thing I'm patient. I'll be back tonight or tomorrow. Be careful—both of you."

After Jason left, Holly asked, "Did I hear the story?"

"Yes, the story of Madeline's twin, remember?"

"I wonder why she's here."

"That's a whole separate mystery. Are you ready to go get your overnight gear?"

"Yes. I'd rather go before it gets dark."

"Do you have anything tasty hiding in your freezer?"

"Probably." Holly giggled.

"I suppose we should get another pet bed too. Marmalade always kicks Mavis out of hers."

"Was that you who left that pile of money on my counter?"

"Yeah. I needed a lot of cat supplies."

"You didn't have to."

"You bought them, and you'll have to replace them. Just use the money for ordering more stuff to give away." Lizzy grinned.

She got a blanket for Mavis and shrugged into her coat. "I'm glad you took me blizzard shopping before you left. I would have been so unprepared."

Holly put on her coat too, still slightly damp from playing in the snow. "It must be hard to imagine until you experience it."

She wound her long hair and stuck it in her cap. "Ready?"

Mavis ran for the door, but Lizzy stopped her with an extended foot. "You stay here with Marmalade. We'll be right back." She heard the barking through the door. "Incorrigible."

"Maybe you should try to call Madeline while I pack. You may need a lot more than a bed."

"Will do—right after I raid your freezer."

More worried than she let on, Lizzy telephoned the hotel as soon as Holly went upstairs. When Mr. Prichard answered, she asked for Madeline.

"Who is this?" he demanded.

"Lizzy. Your neighbor. How are you doing after your fall?"

"Fine. Sprained arm. What do you want with Mad?"

"I'd like to speak with her. Is she there?"

"I think you know she isn't. What do you want?"

Lizzy weighed her possible answers. Madeline seemed to love and trust her husband despite his rough exterior. "Mr. Prichard, did she tell you about Serena?"

"Yer. Then she left."

Yer. That's a new one. His vernacular distracted her momentarily. "I'm worried about her. Cleo showed up at my house today."

Muttered swearing, then silence. After a moment he said, "She wouldn't leave without that cat."

"I think we should call the police."

He sighed heavily. "Can you bring that friend of yours over here?"

She asked for his room number and disconnected, then called Jason. As she was finishing that call, Holly wandered into the kitchen.

"Did you find out anything?"

"Madeline's missing," Lizzy said. "Let's take your things over to my place. You can stay there in case she shows up, and I'll go with Jason to the hotel."

"How will I know it's her and not her sister?"

"Marmalade doesn't like Serena."

"Oh yeah. What do I do if she shows up? Is she dangerous?"

"I don't know. We can ask Jason when he gets here."

It took two trips to get Holly's things and the extra cat supplies across the street. Jason pulled up to the curb and got out of the cruiser to help with the heavy box of cat litter.

"Memories…" Lizzy sang when she caught sight of the three animals sleeping in front of the fire.

Jason chuckled. "Tell me about Madeline."

Repeating the story, Lizzy relayed her plan and Holly's concern. "Is it safe to let her in the house if she shows up?"

"She may not. Text or call if she does. Then we'll decide. Barker's at the hospital with Mrs. Fickle, and Nettle's on call right now. We really need to find a replacement for Rice."

"Why haven't you?"

"It's complicated. Let's get a move on. I'll have Lizzy back here as soon as possible. Keep the door locked."

Holly nodded and saw them out.

⸺⸺⸺ ❦ ⸺⸺⸺

Jason drove to the hotel in silence. He thought again of Pastor Turnbull's words and fought to still his mind. He had never had to deal with so many incidents in such a short period of time and wondered if they could all be connected.

Out of the corner of his eye, he observed his passenger. *I'm glad she's on my side. How does she always end up in the middle of everything?* Breaking the silence, he asked, "How did you find out about Serena?"

"It was the cat."

"But…" He didn't know how to ask.

He pulled into the small hotel parking lot and wondered if Prichard had transportation. "What was the room number?"

"One twenty-two."

Jason was familiar with the hotel's layout since it was the only one in town. He led Lizzy to room 122 and knocked.

Napoleon Prichard opened the door in a dirty T-shirt, thick stubble on his face. His red-tinged eyes shifted back and forth between Jason and Lizzy. "Come in," he mumbled, stepping back.

Lizzy scrunched her nose at the stale smell. Takeout boxes and dirty laundry hinted that Madeline had been absent for some time. Mr. Prichard slouched on the edge of the unmade king-sized bed. "I thought she left me."

"Did you argue?" Lizzy asked.

"I thought she was making it up. I've met her sister, but I never mentioned it. I thought Mad had some kind of mental problem. Like a split personality or something. I even contacted a psychiatrist once."

"So, you confronted her, and it didn't go too well?"

Jason listened, amazed at how effortlessly Lizzy got Prichard to open up.

"She didn't yell. She never does. But she was upset. She told me I needed to pay attention. She was scared."

"Did she say she was scared, or you could just tell?"

"I could tell. We've been together a long time. I thought she was scared because she felt another episode coming on, and I was mad 'cause I thought she was spinning me a tale. I told her she should just be honest with me, and I left the room to clear my head. That was the last I saw her."

"Has she ever disappeared before?"

"No. I thought she finally left me 'cause the cat was gone too. She loves her more than me."

"Finally left you?"

"She's too good for me, always putting up with my crap. I knew she'd leave one of these days."

"When I spoke with her, she was worried about you. Serena's been seen with Lucian Basile. You know him, right?"

Mr. Prichard's ruddy face darkened. "How would he know her? Are you sure it wasn't Mad?"

"I've met them both. They look alike, but there are slight differences."

"Like what? How can I tell them apart?"

Lizzy told him what she had observed. "The biggest difference is how Cleo reacts to them."

"That cat follows Maddy around everywhere."

Leaning toward him from where she had perched on the edge of a chair, Lizzy said, "Serena has been posing as your wife. Do you have any idea what she might be up to? Are you on good terms with Lucian?"

Napoleon shivered. "He's a bad dude. Maddy was always after me to cut ties with him. I'm pretty sure that's the only reason she agreed to move here."

Lizzy glanced at Jason, standing in the corner with his arms crossed. "How were he and Christine connected?"

"She works for him. I think she's his girlfriend."

"Did you know she's been murdered?"

He sat up straight and stared at her with a slack jaw. Jason thought he understood. Too many things were happening at once.

Napoleon swallowed hard. "We have to find Maddy."

"Do you have any idea where we should start?" Jason asked.

"Find Lucian and follow him?"

"Where is he staying?"

Mr. Prichard shook his head. "I don't even know where he lives. He just shows up. I had a phone number, but he changes it every week."

"Does your wife have any other family?"

"Her mom lives in a memory-care home in North Dakota. I don't even know what it's called."

"Where's her phone?" Lizzy asked.

"She must have it. I've tried calling and texting, but she doesn't answer."

"We'll start looking for Lucian. Give some serious thought to what he or Serena might want from you and call me the minute either of them makes contact." Jason handed him a card. Prichard's face had a greenish hue.

Lizzy stood and walked toward him, placing her hand on his shoulder. "We'll do our best," she said gently. "Get yourself cleaned up in case we need your help. And feel free to stop by and see Cleo."

"That cat." He shook his head and swiped at his eyes. "Mad sure loves her." His voice cracked.

Lizzy felt sorry for him. *I really misjudged him.* She followed Jason out of the room, glancing back to see Mr. Prichard drop his head into his hands. His shoulders quaked as she quietly pulled the door shut.

Inside the cruiser, she looked at Jason's face and could see he'd been affected too. "How will we find her? She could be anywhere."

"Not really. Lucian and Serena must be staying somewhere. If not in town, then in Sioux Falls, but it's quite a drive back and forth."

"Only thirty minutes," Lizzy said.

"But think about it. Driving to Sioux Falls for the day is fine, but if they're here every day, what do they do while they're here? Where do they hang out? There's nowhere to hide."

"You have a point. What now?"

"I'll drop you off; then I have to spell Barker."

The hotel was only three blocks from Lizzy's house, at the end of Main Street. As Jason pulled up at the curb, she said, "Let me know when Mrs. Fickle wakes."

"Will do. Let me know if you hear anything."

"Yes, sir." Lizzy winked at him and got out of the cruiser, then he pulled away.

Holly was waiting at the open front door. "What happened? Tell me everything."

"Hold on there, cowgirl. Let me collect my thoughts." Lizzy removed her coat and boots. "How are the cats settling in?"

"See for yourself. They haven't moved an inch. Want some coffee?"

"Yes, please." She grinned and turned to follow Holly to the kitchen, immediately joined by Mavis. "What did you do with Candy?" She looked back to see the kitten stretching and yawning widely. "Just left her in the dust, huh?"

"Arooerer," Mavis said, wagging her tail.

"Okay, here's your coffee. Now spill. No pun intended."

Lizzy sat with her coffee, attempting to ignore Mavis' antics. "I guess it's that time. Just hold on, Mavis." She took a sip.

Mavis whined, ending in a pathetic, cooing sound.

"Are you sure she's not part pigeon?" Holly asked.

"She's something." Lizzy got back up to prepare Mavis' dinner and told Holly about the meeting with Mr. Prichard. "Jason seems to think we'll be able to find her, but I don't know."

"He's very good at his job. He'll find her."

"What do you suppose they want?"

"Maybe Serena wants Mr. Prichard. But why after all these years? And why would Mrs. Fickle's cousin help her?"

Lizzy canted her head to the right. "I hope she's okay."

"Are you getting hungry?"

Right on cue, Lizzy's stomach grumbled. "I guess I am."

"I made a salad and defrosted the lasagna."
"Perfect."

Chapter 21

Fire!

Sitting on an uncomfortable chair in Mrs. Fickle's hospital room, Jason pondered recent events. The constant barrage of incidents was preventing him from following up on any of them. He hadn't been able to organize his thoughts or update the incident board. He thought back to Christine's murder. Holly's fingerprints on the broken glass, the footprints in the spilled cocktail, the number of people who'd been in and out of the room.

Then he turned his mind to Mrs. Fickle and the phenobarbital. That was a controlled substance. A look at Holly's records should show whether any was missing. He was only one person, and he needed help. No matter how much he wanted to reinstate Rice, he knew it was impossible. Her inappropriate behavior couldn't be erased. *I'll start with the clinic in the morning, then decide if I need to make the call.*

He thought some more and changed his mind. *I'm just being stubborn.* He dialed his superior in Sioux Falls and explained the situation.

"I'll send you two officers. Do you need them tonight?"

"Tomorrow's probably fine."

"Don't leave it so long next time. And let's work on filling that position. I'll be there tomorrow, and we'll come up with a plan."

"Yes, sir. Thank you."

He disconnected with a feeling of relief. He remembered the pastor's words once again. *I don't have to do everything myself. I can ask for help.*

Lizzy was quiet during dinner. Holly observed her rapidly changing facial expressions and didn't interrupt whatever was going on in her head. She never knew with Lizzy. She might be thinking about the murder or Madeline or even the plot of her new book.

Which reminded Holly of her own situation. She wondered if Mrs. Prichard's disappearance had anything to do with the murder and if that was going to be pinned on her too. It didn't seem likely, but neither had anything else.

Lizzy looked up when she sighed. "What's wrong? Did I miss something?"

"No, I was just thinking about everything that's happened since Saturday."

"Me too. It doesn't make sense. I think I'll go to bed early if that's okay with you. I feel exhausted."

"That's fine. I'm tired too." Holly's insomnia kept her up at night, but she could nap at odd times. She thought it might be early enough to trick her body for an hour or two.

Lizzy took Mavis outside and set the burglar alarm when they returned. "See you in the morning," she mumbled. Mavis hopped up the stairs behind her.

Holly had her own designated room upstairs, but she put an extra log on the fire and closed the curtains. She stretched out on the sofa with Candy and was lulled to sleep by the crackle of the fire and the kitten's soft purr.

***

Lizzy lay in bed with her eyes open. Mavis curled up behind her knees, and after a while, she felt Marmalade's soft landing on the end of her bed. She puzzled over recent events, relationships, arguments, lies until she fell into a fitful sleep.

She dreamt of Mavis barking at a shadowy villain who was attacking Holly with a knife. Holly's scream morphed into the high-pitched squeal of the burglar alarm.

Waking disoriented, Lizzy turned to find Mavis hysterical and an eerie glow shining through her bedroom window.

She ran to the window and saw flames rising from Holly's clinic. Her pulse skyrocketed as she reached for her phone. She heard sirens but called Jason anyway.

"Schneider," he answered.

"Holly's clinic is on fire."

"I heard. I'm on my way."

"'Kay." Lizzy disconnected and ran downstairs. The front door was standing open, the alarm was blaring, and Holly was gone. Mavis shot past and through the door, surprisingly fast despite her short legs. Lizzy followed in her bedroom slippers. She tripped twice but kept going.

Wearing only sweatpants and a T-shirt, Holly lay unconscious in the snow outside the clinic. The firemen reached her just before Lizzy did, so Lizzy sprinted toward the frenzied barking and howling emanating from the burning structure.

"Stop!" Chief Byron shouted. "Stop her!"

Two volunteer firefighters gave chase as she tore through the clinic to the recovery bay. She fumbled with the first lock, pushing the firefighters away. "If you want me out of here, help me."

Six dogs and a cat frantically tried to escape as Lizzy and the volunteers quickly unlocked the cages.

As the terrified dogs ran for the exit, Mavis' barking rose above the commotion outside. Deep gashes on Lizzy's arms and chest bled as she held on to the struggling cat, her eyes blurry and tearing from the smoke. She wheezed and coughed as she stumbled from the building and was led to the open back of an ambulance and urged to sit next to Holly. Someone placed an oxygen mask over her face and a blanket around her shoulders, and asked if they could take the cat.

Lizzy wrapped her arms around the feline and shook her head, quaking as the shock set in.

Holly sat next to her and cried. "Did you save them all?"

"I think so."

"I can't believe you did that. You might have died."

"Maybe. What happened to you?"

"I don't know. I'm so cold."

Lizzy eyed Holly's T-shirt and bare feet. "You're nuts."

"So are you. I love you so much for what you did. You're my hero." Big fat tears flowed from her eyes. She sniffed loudly and said, "That's Gray, by the way. He got hit by a car last week."

That was it. Lizzy couldn't stop her tears. She didn't even try. She hugged the cat and felt his sharp claws.

Half considering a change of profession, Jason approached the ambulance. Holly and Lizzy sat on the bay, crying. Mavis sat several yards away, surrounded by a group of shivering dogs. He felt powerless. He wanted to yell at someone, to hit something, but he knew that wouldn't help.

Lizzy removed the oxygen mask and coughed. She looked up at him with red, unfocused eyes, and his heart clenched. Lizzy never cried. Whatever happened had affected her to the core. "Can we go inside?" she asked, her teeth chattering. "It's cold out here."

"Yes. What do you want to do with the dogs?"

"They can come too."

Jason glanced at Holly, surmising she was in shock. Her face was very pale. "Can you walk?" he asked her.

"We should take her to the hospital," one of the paramedics said.

"Why don't you let her get warmed up first? She's not even wearing shoes."

"I don't think she can walk on her own. Can you ride on my back?" she asked gently.

Holly nodded and put her arms around the paramedic's neck when she turned and bent her knees.

Lizzy and Jason accompanied them, followed by Mavis and a parade of dogs. He glanced back when Mavis barked twice and sat on the porch. The other dogs stood and waited. He watched as Lizzy carried the cat she was holding upstairs, then returned for Marmalade and Candy. When she descended with a pile of blankets, he saw the bloody gashes on her neck and arms. *Those are going to hurt*, he thought.

Mavis stood and led the dogs inside. *I must be imagining things.* He shut the door and put another log on the fire.

The paramedic checked Holly's vital signs and helped Lizzy wrap her in blankets. "I'll be back. Don't let her sleep."

Jason wrapped Lizzy in blankets after she sat next to Holly. She smelled of smoke and her hair was singed, making him shudder at what might have happened to her. Mavis jumped up beside her and leaned against her leg.

"You're such a good puppy," she said, stroking her ears.

Jason perched on the coffee table in front of her. "Can you tell me what happened after you called me?"

She told him what she could. Holly stared into the fire.

"What possessed you to run into a burning building?"

"I didn't know what happened to Holly, but I knew why she was there. She was there to save her patients, and if she couldn't, then I was going to. I would have died before I let them burn."

Jason saw Holly's tears and didn't know what to say.

"Holly? Did you see anyone before you were knocked out?"

"I-I don't think so. All I can remember is seeing the flames and hearing the dogs. I panicked."

"How did the fire start?" Lizzy whispered.

"There'll be an investigation, but it wasn't an accident."

She shivered.

He didn't want to leave them alone, so he called Doc Steve, who arrived shortly, along with Dottie.

The doctor checked both Lizzy's and Holly's vitals and told Jason he could release the ambulance. "We'll stay here for a while, and I'll keep an eye on them."

Chapter 22

Here Comes the Cavalry

Along for moral support, Dottie brought pastries. Lizzy took one look at the box and shuddered.

"Don't be like that. You'll put me out of business."

"I can't help it. What time is it?"

"It's two. What are you doing with all these dogs?"

"They were in the clinic. Who would do that? It's just sick."

Dottie frowned and glanced at her husband. "Maybe the same person who killed Christine?"

Lizzy didn't respond. Dottie was right. Giving someone cyanide to drink was also very sick. She opened the curtains and turned off the lights, watching the firefighters battle the flames. The ever-present wind had shifted. It blew eastward toward the shops, threatening the entire block. The edge of Holly's house, adjacent to the west, smoldered but remained intact, the interior stone walls preventing a fast burn.

"Could you close the curtains?" Holly asked. "I can't watch."

Lizzy closed them and turned the lights back on. Then she texted Jason and told him to send the firefighters over when they needed a break. Steve and the dogs dozed. Dottie, Holly, and Lizzy sat quietly, waiting for news.

As the sun rose, the firefighters arrived one at a time. Knocking politely and removing their boots, they followed Lizzy into the kitchen for a hot drink and one of Dottie's pastries. Mavis, worn out from her earlier efforts, snored softly on the sofa. Lizzy didn't ask questions. She knew Jason would fill her in. She merely did what she could to support the brave townsfolk who had been working through the night.

Following the last one outside, Chief Byron, she stood on her porch and surveyed the damage. The real estate office next to the clinic was destroyed, but all the other businesses had been saved. The exterior of Holly's home, blackened and soggy, stood tall on the corner. Many of their neighbors stood outside in coats and boots, some of them sporting nightclothes underneath. A couple of the women saw Lizzy and looked like they might approach, but Jason, wiping his brow with his coat sleeve, beat them to it.

"How's Holly?" he called on his way across the intersection.

"They all fell asleep."

"I thought Doc Steve was going to keep an eye on her."

"He was the first to go." Lizzy winked.

"Got any leftover refreshments?"

"Yes. Come on in."

They entered quietly and sat at the kitchen table with coffee and the remaining pastries. "Have you found out anything else?" Lizzy asked.

"Just that it was definitely arson. Most of the snow is packed hard now, but we found a footprint around back that looks like the same size as some of the footprints at the murder scene. It's hard to be sure because it was made with a boot."

"I was thinking. In mystery novels, the detective often looks at the victim's life and relationships to discover the motive. Maybe we should be taking a closer look at Christine."

"Maybe." He had those pinchy lines between his brows again. "I asked for help from Sioux Falls. We have a meeting at ten."

Jason remained at Lizzy's until it was time for him to spell Barker. Mavis had waddled into the kitchen and made her presence known. When they walked him out, Lizzy gave him a hug and wished him luck.

So tired he could hardly think, he hoped the additional manpower would allow him to get some rest.

He relieved Barker, settling himself in the uncomfortable visitor's chair they placed behind the door to Mrs. Fickle's room. His eyes closed involuntarily, and he dozed, waking when a nursing assistant entered to take her patient's vitals. To his surprise, Mrs. Fickle was conscious.

"Hello, Jason. How long have you been here?"

"I just arrived. How are you feeling?"

"Not my best, to be honest. The doctor said I was poisoned."

The nursing assistant left, promising to bring food, and Mrs. Fickle's eyes drifted shut again. A tap on the door heralded Lucian's arrival. He tiptoed into the room and, without noticing Jason, approached the bed.

Mrs. Fickle's eyes opened, and Jason put a finger to his lips, hoping she wouldn't give his presence away.

She looked at Lucian. "What are you doing here?"

"Just checking on my favorite cousin. Have you decided to cooperate?"

"I don't know what you mean."

"Don't play dumb. You know what I want."

"I really don't. You seem to think I have something I don't."

He leaned over her and snarled. "You've seen what can happen to you if you're stubborn. Just give me what I want, and I'll disappear."

"Are you saying you put me in the hospital?"

"What do you think?"

His unpleasant chuckle made Jason clench his fists. *Was that enough of a confession?*

"Maybe next time you won't be so lucky."

Yep. There it was. Jason stood. "Mr. Basile, you are under arrest for attempted murder."

Lucian swung around to face Jason, his mouth open.

"What are you talking about? I didn't kill nobody."

"No, as you said, she got lucky this time. Hands behind your back." Jason snapped on the handcuffs and calmly recited the Miranda warning while Lucian argued and blustered. As he escorted Lucian out of the room, Jason turned back toward Mrs. Fickle. "Rest and get well. He won't be bothering you anymore."

At the station, Jason asked Nettle to process the intake and accompany Lucian to the interview room. He joined them at the white plastic table in the otherwise-empty room. Looking across the table at Lucian Basile, he didn't see much resemblance to Sage Fickle other than his height. He was considerably younger, for one thing, swarthier, heavier, and bald.

"Where is Serena?" Jason asked.

"Who's Serena? And what's this got to do with Sage?"

Jason shrugged. "Okay, where's Madeline?"

"How should I know? Are you just on a fishing expedition? I want my lawyer."

Deciding to try another tack, Jason asked, "Where'd you get the cyanide?"

"Cyanide?" Lucian's voice rose with his heavy eyebrows. "Dude, you have got to be kidding. I don't mess with no cyanide."

"How did you poison Sage?"

"I didn't know she was poisoned. I was just trying to scare her."

"What is it you want from her?"

"What I want right now is my lawyer. I'm not saying another word until he gets here."

Jason stood and nodded at Nettle. "Let him have his phone call and put him in the holding cell. Our meeting's in an hour."

Although he was a small fastidious man, Chief Montgomery had presence.

He strode into the station, followed by two crisply uniformed sergeants, took one look at Jason, and said, "You look terrible."

Jason hung his head.

Appearing at his side and placing a hand on his shoulder, Barker said, "He hasn't slept in days, sir. We're up to our necks."

"So I gather. Where shall we meet?"

"My office," Jason said. "The incident board's in there, although it hasn't been updated."

"Lead the way, Captain."

Once they were seated, Nettle joined them and sat near the door.

"All right, Schneider. Let's have an update."

Jason led them through the incidents and the evidence up to that morning's arrest. Barker added the most up-to-date information to the board as Jason spoke.

Chief Montgomery's eyebrows drew ever closer together. When Jason stopped speaking, he said, "You should have called sooner. What conclusions have you reached?"

Shaking his head, Jason said, "None. I haven't had a moment to think."

"Why haven't you arrested Holly? Is that a conflict of interest?"

"No, sir. I didn't arrest her after the murder because the evidence was circumstantial, and I couldn't see a motive. After the poisoning, I wished I had, just to have her out of it."

"A veterinarian's drug was used in the poisoning, and we only have her word as to where the food came from. Yet you still didn't arrest her."

"She left it on her best friend's doorstep."

"You know better than that."

"I suppose. But before we could thoroughly investigate, one of her neighbors disappeared and her clinic burned down."

"Perhaps she burned it down to prevent you from finding the drugs were missing."

"Someone knocked her out."

"You have medical evidence?"

"Yes, sir."

"With that amount of evidence pointing at one suspect, it needs to be investigated. Let's assign Sergeant Rodriguez to that so there won't be any doubt."

"Yes, sir."

"Now about today's arrest. Is it likely this man is involved?"

"It's hard to say. He did claim responsibility in the hospital but then recanted when I questioned him."

"And the missing woman?"

"I have no idea how she fits in, but in a town this size, it's likely she does."

"Sergeant Tate can get onto that. Nettle, you man the desk. Schneider, you and Barker will be more useful once you've had some sleep."

Jason wanted to argue, but he knew the chief was right. He nodded respectfully. "I'll be back in about five hours."

"No, you need a full eight hours. I don't want to see you back here until tomorrow morning."

"But, sir..."

"You heard me. We need that brain of yours working at full speed. Get out of here."

Jason sighed. "Yes, sir."

Chapter 23

Enter Rodriguez

Holly, accompanied by seven yapping dogs, opened Lizzy's front door to a stranger. Her first impression was a mouthful of very white teeth. Dressed in a police uniform, the man seemed tall, but then Holly stood only slightly over five feet. His voice was unusually deep when he introduced himself as Sergeant Rodriguez and asked to speak with Holly Schneider.

"I'm Holly. This is my friend, Lizzy." She gestured toward Lizzy, who had approached the door behind her. "How can I help you?"

"I'd like to speak to you alone."

"You two can sit in here by the fire," Lizzy said. "I can go into the kitchen. Would you like some coffee?"

"No, thank you. I think it would be better if you go upstairs if you don't mind."

Holly could see that Lizzy did mind, but she got herself a cup of coffee and called Mavis, who was busy sniffing the sergeant's pant legs. She shrugged and continued upstairs.

Holly turned and surveyed her guest. "Why don't you have a seat and tell me what this is about?"

He waited until she sat on the sofa, then sat on the loveseat to her right. "Your brother requested assistance from the Sioux Falls police department, and his superior assigned me to investigate your role in recent events."

"Isn't that already documented?"

"Not entirely. I'd like to start at the beginning and go over it with you."

Holly sat silently, wondering where he was headed.

"Let's start with the murder of Christine Luc. How well did you know the victim?"

"We went to school together, but I haven't seen her for ten years."

"Would you say you were friends?"

"No, not really. I don't think we really knew each other after all that time."

"Tell me about how you found her body."

"I didn't. Lizzy and Rice found her."

"Did you notice anything strange about the body?"

Holly tilted her head. "I didn't see it."

"Then why were your footprints in the spilled drink?"

"Obviously, I was in the room at some point. So were several other people. But I didn't see a body. If I had, I would have told someone."

"Your fingerprints were also on the glass she drank from. How did you get her to drink it?"

"Drink what?"

"Whatever you put in the glass."

"I wasn't in the habit of socializing with her. I didn't give her anything to drink. Dottie said nothing but bottled water upstairs."

"And you're a rule follower, right?"

"Yes."

"Do you have anyone who can vouch for your whereabouts at the time of death?"

"I don't know. What was the time of death?"

Rodriguez frowned and looked through the file in his lap. They hadn't included the autopsy results. "Let's move on to the poisoning of your neighbor. Mrs. Fickle? She was staying here at the time, I believe?"

"Yes. How is she?"

"I don't know, ma'am. Tell me how you came to be in possession of phenobarbital."

"I'm a veterinarian. All vets have it. We use it for pet euthanasia."

"So you're comfortable taking lives."

Already slightly annoyed, Holly took umbrage at his words. "I'd like to speak with your superior."

"I'm afraid that's not possible at this time."

"You can ask questions, but it's not okay to cast aspersions on my profession. As a Doctor of Veterinary Medicine, I can assure you that I uphold my oath and do not wander around killing animals for fun." She could feel the heat in her face and knew she was bright red. "We're done here unless you're prepared to arrest me."

<hr>

Holly's voice rose in pitch and volume, prompting Lizzy to investigate. She descended the stairs and asked, "Is everything okay?"

Rodriguez started to say yes, but Holly, on a roll, continued her diatribe.

Lizzy laid her hand on Holly's arm and waited for her to pause. "Perhaps the sergeant would like to apologize for his careless wording."

Holly stared at him.

"No, I don't think so. You can answer my questions in a civil manner, or we can continue this interview at the station."

"Let's go."

"I can assure you that your brother won't be there to cover for you."

Holly stood and left the room. Rodriguez moved to follow her, but Lizzy stopped him. "I think you should leave. Send someone else or return with a warrant. You're no longer welcome here."

Mavis growled, her hackles rising.

Lizzy escorted Rodriguez to the door and locked it behind him. There would be backlash. Deciding to be proactive, she dialed the police station and asked for the chief.

"May I ask who's calling?" asked an unfamiliar male voice.

Hoping to sound more important than she was, she said, "This is Elizabeth Hornwhistle."

A pause. "The writer?"

"Yes." He knew who she was?

"Just one moment, please."

There was a click, and after a moment a smooth, congenial voice said, "Good afternoon, Ms. Hornwhistle. This is Chief Montgomery. How can I help you?"

"I'd like to lodge a complaint."

After a moment of silence, the chief asked, "Are you in Harperstown, ma'am?"

"Yes. I moved here in December—somewhat incognito, if you know what I mean."

"Oh um, yes, of course." He cleared his throat. "So, about your complaint?"

Lizzy watched Mavis as she stood stiff legged over Candy, growling at a one-eared Doberman. The Doberman lay down, and Mavis curled up around Candy, her eyes remaining open. The protector.

"I have a friend staying with me. Her family has been a great benefactor since I've been in Harperstown, and she has been through some major trauma recently. Her business burnt to the ground, and her home was damaged."

"I'm aware of the situation."

"This afternoon, one of your officers came to my home to interview her. That was fine. He interrupted my work and sent me upstairs. That was okay too, I suppose. But during his interview with Ms. Schneider, he... crossed a line, Chief Montgomery."

"How?" The chief's voice was suddenly sharp.

"It's hard to explain to someone who doesn't understand Holly's deep dedication to her profession, but Sergeant Rodriguez basically said that since Holly occasionally performs pet euthanasia, she wouldn't have a problem taking a life.

He sat in my living room, surrounded by wounded dogs we rescued from the fire, and inferred that she doesn't care about her patients or life in general. When I came downstairs to calm her, he refused to apologize and threatened to take her to the station. Then when she agreed to go, he said her brother wouldn't be able to 'cover for her' this time. He was ugly and confrontational."

After another moment, the chief said, "I know Holly. Do you think she would be willing to continue the interview if I accompany Rodriguez and he apologizes?"

"I imagine so. As far as I know, she was compliant up to that point."

"I believe Sergeant Rodriguez is waiting to see me. Expect us in about an hour."

"Thank you, Chief." Lizzy disconnected and let out a deep breath. She ran her hand through her singed hair and glanced at the dogs lying peacefully in front of the fire.

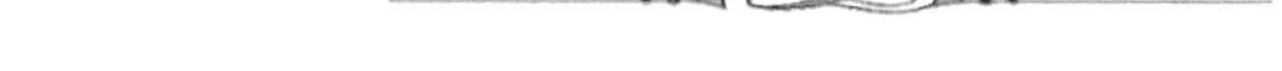

Grateful for Lizzy, Holly knew she wasn't at her best. She had overreacted, and that was probably what Rodriguez had been aiming for. He was looking to hit a nerve. But the events of the past week had been too much. Lizzy made her a sandwich and sat to eat with her, but she didn't have much of an appetite. Mavis stared at her and whined. Absently giving her bits of sandwich, Holly said, "We should probably take the dogs out."

"Yeah. Have you contacted their owners?"

"The computer and all my records burned." She felt numb. Everything was gone.

"Do you have a backup?"

"I usually back everything up once a week, but I've been so busy. I asked my mom to contact people."

"Let's take them outside and worry about that later."

They didn't have coats for all the dogs, but Lizzy put Mavis' on. "Help us out, puppy. We're going to need some assistance."

Mavis barked at the other dogs, who rose reluctantly and followed her outside. She did her business, then trotted the perimeter, barking and wagging her tail.

"They seem to do whatever she tells them to. Isn't that weird?" Lizzy asked.

"Maybe it's because she brought them in from the cold after the fire," Holly suggested. She really had no idea. Mavis was one of a kind.

"Okay, everybody inside," Lizzy called.

The dogs, busy sniffing and playing in the snow, completely ignored her. "Mavis? Let's go inside," she said.

Holly shook her head as she watched Mavis run for the porch, barking. She sat by the front door where the other dogs joined her. "So weird," she said.

"Here come the police," Lizzy said. "I hope they're nicer this time."

"Rodriguez doesn't look particularly happy."

Sergeant Rodriguez wasn't smiling when he got out of his cruiser and rounded the hood to open the passenger door. The chief, on the other hand, smiled broadly. "Holly, my girl. It's good to see you. And this must be Ms. Hornwhistle." He held out his hand for Lizzy to shake. "My wife and I read your books and discuss them over dinner."

Lizzy shook his hand and returned his smile. "I'm glad you enjoy them."

Chief Montgomery glanced at Rodriguez, who clenched his fists. "Ms. Schneider, Doctor, I apologize for my poor choice of words during our earlier interview. I hope we can make a fresh start." He spoke through gritted teeth.

"I apologize too," Holly said. "I've had a rough week, and I probably overreacted."

He relaxed slightly at her words.

"Why don't we get these dogs inside and you can get back to it," Lizzy said brightly.

The chief accepted coffee and permitted Lizzy to remain, provided she didn't comment.

The interview proceeded smoothly until they reached the part about the fire. Holly hadn't received a final report, nor had she thoroughly processed her loss. Rodriguez, once again lacking any kind of emotional sensitivity, began insinuating that she burned down her own clinic. Lizzy took Holly's hand and said, "Chief?"

"Stop there, Rodriguez," he said. "Despite whatever you have running through your own head, you have here a young lady who lost her place of business. She was injured and has a houseful of patients she almost lost to the fire. Where trauma is involved, we must strive for tact and empathy."

"But sir…"

"No buts. Keep your personal thoughts and suspicions to yourself for now."

Rodriguez scowled, and the chief continued. "This is where you might be able to help us out, Ms. Hornwhistle. Holly was already staying here. Is that correct?"

"Yes."

"Why is that?"

"Jason thought she might be in danger."

He nodded. "He was correct, apparently. The fire was started in the middle of the night. Were you two still up?"

"I was sleeping," Lizzy said. "Holly suffers from insomnia."

The chief shifted his focus to Holly. "You were awake?"

"I had dozed but heard Mavis barking upstairs."

"Mavis?"

"Lizzy's dog. The miniature dachshund." Holly pointed.

Mavis barked and wagged her tail, as if on cue.

"Anyway, I saw a strange glow from outside and looked through the window. I panicked. All I could think about was the animals trapped inside."

"You ran for the clinic, and then what happened?"

"I don't know. I remember flames coming out the door and windows and wondering how to get in. Then I felt like my head exploded."

"You were right behind her?" he asked Lizzy, and she told him her version of the story.

"Based on the reports we've received, I don't see any way Holly could have set that fire, certainly without shoes. Nor can I see any possible benefit to burning down her own place of business. She could have just staged a theft if she wanted to get rid of evidence."

Holly wasn't sure who he was addressing, but she was relieved to hear his logical assessment. She thought Rodriguez was about to blow.

"And how could she have knocked herself out and given herself a concussion?" Lizzy asked.

"That too."

As the interview wound down, pet parents arrived with condolences and gratitude. The chief, and thus Rodriguez, sat and observed. When the cat and four of the dogs had been collected, Chief Montgomery stood. "I'm truly sorry for your loss, my dear. It's evident how much your customers and their pets love you."

"Thank you, Chief." Holly smiled through her tears. "I don't think I could have gone on if they... Lizzy saved them." She began to sob in earnest, and Lizzy held her as she cried. All the trauma and stress poured from her, leaving her feeling weak and shaky. The police left, and only Lizzy remained, holding her quietly.

Chapter 24

Madeline Returns

Jason was summoned to his office the next morning. Chief Montgomery sat in his chair, studying the incident board. "Are you feeling rested?"

"Much better. Thank you, sir."

"I suppose you heard about our interview with Holly."

"No, I haven't."

"Sit down and let's have a chat."

Jason sat on the hard wooden chair he reserved for visitors. He listened carefully to the chief's recap of the initial interview, Lizzy's phone call, and his final conclusions.

"You might have sent someone other than Rodriguez. Was she very upset?"

"It might have been cathartic. It might also have been good for Rodriguez. I hope he learned something. For such an up-and-coming young officer, he has zero people skills."

Curious, Jason asked, "What did you think of Lizzy?"

"Ah. Lizzy, is it? An interesting woman. And a good friend to your sister. I admire her fierce loyalty."

Jason admired that trait as well.

"My second bit of news is that Tate found the missing woman. Madeline Prichard."

"Really? Where was she?"

"She showed up at the hotel and claims she doesn't remember."

"Are you convinced it's Madeline and not her sister?"

"What's this about a sister?"

Jason explained. "We should take them to Lizzy's and ask the cat. She's the only one who knows for sure."

The chief wiped his forehead with a handkerchief. "I can certainly see why you've been having trouble here. I wanted to ask you about Mr. Basile too. He and his lawyer are making a lot of noise. And also, what's this on the incident board about sabotage?"

Jason slumped in his chair.

"I understand. I do. Maybe between the six of us, we can get it sorted. Tell me about Mr. Basile, and let's get him off your plate."

Barker knocked and stuck his head around the door. "Mrs. Fickle is being released. I'm going to give her a ride to Lizzy's."

"Another houseguest?"

"Yes, sir. She lives next door but was worried about Mr. Basile."

"And she was staying at Ms. Hornwhistle's when she was poisoned?"

"Yes."

The chief glanced at Jason, who said, "Mr. Basile insinuated he was responsible for poisoning her when he threatened her in the hospital."

"Do you think he's responsible?"

"No… But he broke into her house and threatened her, and he's somehow connected to the Prichards and the murder victim. He's not clean."

"Then we'll hang on to him. Go ahead, Barker. We'll organize new assignments as we proceed."

Barker left, and the chief said, "Just one more question. How about the sabotage? What does that mean?"

"As far as I can tell, it had nothing to do with our primary case. It did fall into the same time frame, however, and caused a lot of chaos. I haven't had an opportunity to speak with the suspects and their families because—"

"You had to prioritize. So, what happened?"

Jason explained what was happening around the time of the murder and the statements he had obtained about the boys' activities, leaving the chief shaking his head.

He wiped his forehead again. "You should have called sooner." Gazing at Jason he said, "This is your case—or cases, perhaps. How would you like to proceed?"

"I need to let go. Maybe Tate can interview the boys and their parents. They need to understand the results of their actions, and they may have observed something pertinent."

"Good. Tate and Barker can go together."

"I'd like you to go with me when I take the Prichards to Lizzy's house, if you don't mind. And you can meet Mrs. Fickle."

The chief smiled.

"Rodriguez and Nettle can deal with Lucian and his lawyer."

"Very good. Let's wait for Barker to return and have a brief meeting."

Arriving at the hotel unannounced, Jason knocked politely on the door of room 122. Prichard, when he answered the door, looked like a different man. He was freshly showered and shaven and wore a clean shirt.

"Hello, Mr. Prichard. I'm told Madeline has returned."

"Yes. I'm so relieved." Napoleon's eyes flicked back and forth nervously.

"This is Chief Montgomery, visiting from Sioux Falls. We'd like to take you over to Lizzy's to get Cleo. I'm sure your wife misses her, and Lizzy's been hosting quite a few critters since the fire."

"The fire?"

"Didn't you hear? The animal clinic burned down."

"How terrible. Of course we'll take Cleo off her hands. I think that neighborhood must be cursed." He turned from the door and hollered, "Mad! We need to go with Captain Schneider to get the cat."

Madeline rounded the corner from the bathroom, brushing her hair. "Can't you just go? I'm so tired."

"You know she hates me. Get your coat."

She looked exactly the same as Jason remembered, but Prichard was making crazy eyes at him every time she wasn't looking.

"I hear you have amnesia," Jason said as they got into the cruiser.

"I don't know if it's amnesia. I just can't remember where I've been." She pulled her coat close and leaned against Prichard in the back seat. Napoleon stared straight ahead.

Lizzy was expecting them. She opened the door to a cacophony of barking before Jason could knock. "Hi. Welcome back, Madeline. We were all so worried. I'm afraid Cleo doesn't like our canine boarders, so she's been staying upstairs." She hung their coats while they removed their boots, then said, "Come on up."

Mavis led the way, tail wagging.

Mrs. Fickle waved from the sofa.

"Where's Holly?" Jason asked.

"She's in with the cats. We've been taking turns." Lizzy opened the bedroom door, and Madeline sped by her and scooped up her cat.

Except it wasn't her cat.

Marmalade fought to get out of her grasp. She clawed her and bit her hand, finally escaping under the bed.

"Where's Madeline?" Lizzy asked.

"I don't know what you're talking about."

"We all know about you, Serena, so you might as well tell us," Jason said.

She stared at him, then looked at Mr. Prichard. "I don't understand. Tell them it's me, Nap."

"Maddy finally told me about you. Where is she?"

"Lizzy, you know me. I came here to see Cleo right after Nap's accident."

"Yes, I saw you with Cleo, and I saw Madeline with her too. You are definitely not Madeline."

Seeming to transform before their very eyes, Serena's soft, eager-to-please version of Madeline changed to stone, her cold hard face betraying her character.

"Where is my wife?" Mr. Prichard demanded.

"I have no idea."

"You knew she was gone, or you wouldn't have come to the hotel."

"That is true." Serena's smile sent chills up Jason's spine. He took out his handcuffs. "You can come with us until you decide to cooperate."

She quickly backed away from him, turning toward the door and elbowing her way past Lizzy and Mr. Prichard. Then she tried to run, but tripped over Mavis, who stood strategically in the doorway.

"I hate animals," she spat out as Mr. Prichard took her arm and helped her up.

***

Jason told the chief and Prichard he'd send Nettle back to give them a ride, then left to transport Serena to the station.

Napoleon was distraught. "I didn't think she was Maddy, but I wasn't sure. That's why I called you."

"You did the right thing," Lizzy said. "Cleo doesn't lie. Come on downstairs, and I'll get you a drink."

"I'll stay up here with Marmalade. She's pretty upset too," Holly said.

The chief followed Lizzy and Mr. Prichard downstairs, where Lizzy introduced him to Mrs. Fickle.

"It's a pleasure to meet you," he said. "I've heard so much about you."

"Please call me Sage." She smiled with her crooked tooth and smoothed her long braid.

"Only if you call me Edgar."

Oh boy. Mr. Fickle better look out. Mr. Fickle was in jail for accepting and reselling stolen goods from Lucian.

Lizzy took Mr. Prichard into the kitchen and offered him a seat. "What would you like? Something fruity or something that burns going down?"

"I'll take the burn."

Lizzy retrieved a bottle of whiskey and two shot glasses from the cupboard. She poured them each a shot and handed him one. "To neighbors," she said, lifting her glass.

"To friends." He lifted his. "I won't forget this." He tossed back the shot and shuddered.

When Nettle arrived, Napoleon was a little unsteady on his feet. Nettle scowled at Lizzy, but she and Mrs. Fickle waved cheerfully from the porch as the chief helped Nap to the cruiser.

"Pompous jerk," Lizzy mumbled as she shut the door.

"Who, dear?"

"Nettle, of course."

"Oh, he's harmless, just not too bright. I really like that Edgar. Very charming." She grinned. "May I have a little toot of that whiskey? It smells lovely."

"Is that medically advisable?"

"Yes. I'm right as rain now."

"It's on the kitchen table. Let me run up and see if Holly wants to join us."

When she returned with Holly, Mrs. Fickle was on her second or third. She danced gracefully around the kitchen, Mavis chasing her long, swirling skirt.

Lizzy and Holly joined her, dancing around the table until they collapsed in their chairs, laughing.

"I needed that," Holly said.

Mavis said, "Rowooherer," and Lizzy glanced at the clock.

"Time stands still for no dog. Dinner time."

"Patty!" she called. "George!" The three-legged poodle and a tubby corgi ran into the kitchen.

"We'll have to get you some more food," Holly said. "We can't just run across the street anymore."

"I ordered some from Amazon as soon as I saw how many guests we had. It should get here tomorrow."

"You always amaze me. I'll go up and feed the cats."

"Has Marmalade recovered?"

"Yes, she's fine. She sure hates Serena though."

Chapter 25

Mystery Patient

A call came through from Dr. Steve as Jason was driving Serena to the station. He was torn. He wanted to interview her as soon as possible, but Steve was anxious for his help. Confiding in Barker, he said, "Sit in the hall, and if Lucian and Serena start talking, warn them you're recording their conversation. I don't want them comparing notes."

"Got it. Where will you be?"

"I have an interview with a mystery patient. I'll be back."

Steve was waiting for him when he arrived at the hospital and explained the circumstances surrounding the patient. "The farmer who found her said she was unconscious and nearly frozen, no coat or identification of any kind."

"Why didn't he call an ambulance?"

"He and his wife are living off grid. No telephone and no vehicle other than his tractor. Apparently, he had some challenges getting her back to the house, and then he helped his wife stave off hypothermia. It was dark by then, so he waited until morning to drive the tractor to his nearest neighbor's house and asked him to call me."

"How was she when you arrived?"

"She needed emergency medical attention. I called for an ambulance. She's conscious now but still confused."

When Jason entered the patient's room behind Doc Steve, he stopped and stared. Lying on the bed, looking pale and weak, was Serena. It couldn't be. He had just left her at the station, so she had to be Madeline. The resemblance was uncanny. Even in her disheveled state, she was identical to her sister.

"Good evening. I'm Captain Jason Schneider from the Harperstown police department."

"Harperstown. Yes, that's it." She repeated the name, rolling it around in her mouth. "We've been living in Harperstown."

"Who's we?" Jason asked gently.

"My husband and I. Nap. Where is he?"

"He's been looking for you."

"Cleo. Is Cleo okay?"

"Yes. She's with Lizzy."

Madeline nodded. "She likes Lizzy."

"Do you remember your name?"

"Madeline." She paused. "Madeline Prichard."

"What's the last thing you remember, Madeline?"

"I was in a car."

"Were you driving?"

"No, I don't think so. We only have one car. I don't drive much."

"Was Nap driving?"

She blinked a few times, then said, "No. It was a woman." She shook her head. "I don't remember."

Steve nudged Jason. "Don't push her," he said under his breath.

Jason nodded as he continued. "Were you afraid?"

"No, we were going for coffee."

Huh. Weird. "It was nice to meet you, Madeline. I'll let Lizzy and your husband know you're here."

"Thank you, Captain."

Jason followed Steve out of the room.

"That's the most we've gotten out of her so far," Steve said. "Do you know her?"

"I don't, but I just arrested her twin sister."

"Was it the sister driving?"

Twisting his neck and head to the right in a slow half shake, Jason said, "I don't think so. She said she wasn't scared."

"She's afraid of her sister?"

"I'm not sure, but from what I've heard, they aren't on good terms." He glanced at his watch. "I need to get back to the station. Let me know if she remembers anything else."

"You'll notify her husband?"

"Yes. Do you want me to escort him here? Or have him wait until morning? He's been extremely worried."

"Just let him know. We'll try to accommodate him."

Jason nodded and shook his hand. "Stay in touch."

On his way outside, he called Lizzy and explained the situation. "I don't know how he'll react, and I don't want him bursting into the hospital like a bull."

"Why don't you swing by and pick me up? We can go talk to him in person," she said.

"Be there in fifteen." He disconnected with a sigh of relief.

As Jason suspected, Napoleon was throwing on his coat and ready to race to the hospital immediately. Lizzy asked him to have a seat and listen to the rest of the story. "She's very weak and doesn't remember what happened," she said. "The doctors are trying to keep her calm and allow her to regain her memory naturally."

"But she remembers me, right?"

"When Captain Schneider mentioned Harperstown, it seemed to jog her memory. She asked about you and Cleo."

Napoleon let out a deep breath and hunched over with his elbows on his knees. "When can I see her?"

"You can go tonight, but it might be better to let her rest and visit her tomorrow morning."

"I won't sleep until I see her. You're sure she's not Serena?"

"Serena's in custody, and Madeline has been in the hospital for two days."

"I have to go now. I'll try to stay calm."

Lizzy glanced at Jason. He nodded and said, "Just remember it's after visiting hours and other patients besides Madeline need their rest. I don't want to hear that you caused a ruckus."

⁕

Silent on the way home, Lizzy puzzled over how Madeline ended up nearly frozen in the middle of nowhere. And why?

When they pulled up in front of her house, she asked, "Are you going back to work?"

"No. I've been told I need my rest, so I'll start fresh in the morning. Plus, Harvey's been acting out. I've been neglecting him."

"Bring him over if you need to. Mavis always enjoys his company."

"Thanks." He smiled at her as she got out of the car and waved him on his way.

Holly and Mavis were waiting for her. Mavis stood at the door, wagging her tail, and Lizzy knew she'd been there the entire time she was gone.

"Have you been a good girl?" Lizzy attempted to pet her head and was rewarded with a lifted snout and a damp palm. "Where are Patty and George?"

"Their pet parents picked them up while you were gone," Holly said from the sofa. "How did it go?"

"Okay, I think. Mr. Prichard went to the hospital, but hopefully he'll be on his best behavior."

"Mavis has better manners."

"Sometimes." Lizzy chuckled. "You want a last trip outside, puppy? I'm beat."

Mavis barked once and danced in a circle.

"I'll come too," Holly said. "I wonder what Barker's been up to. I haven't seen him since before the fire. You don't think he suspects me?"

After a short struggle, Lizzy got a wriggling Mavis into her coat. "Of course not. He's probably just busy. The chief's been handing out assignments, right? Has he texted?"

Holly got her coat on and opened the door for the little dog. "He has. A couple of times. No excuses, just how're you doing, miss you, that kind of thing."

"Well, that's something." She watched Mavis rooting around in the snow. It was softer than before, and Lizzy was looking forward to spring. "Is it going to get warm soon?"

Holly frowned. "How did we get from Steve to the weather? No. Forget I asked." She shook her head. "Warm is very subjective."

Lizzy sighed. That probably meant it was going to be a while. Mavis assumed the position and remained for thirteen seconds. Lizzy counted. "All right, girl. Let's get inside. It's cold out here."

Upstairs, she applied a light coating of antibiotic ointment to her still-healing gashes. She hoped Gray was recovering well. *Who knew I would like cats so much? Or dogs for that matter.* She smiled at Mavis, jumping around on her mattress, waiting impatiently. "I'm kind of afraid to go to sleep," she told her. "I don't know what's going to wake me up lately."

"Ahrooherer."

"At least you're here with me." Lizzy hugged her and kissed the top of her head. "Let me just get my pj's on, and we'll go sleepy."

Snuggled under the blankets with Mavis behind her knees, Lizzy lay awake for a long time, thinking. She had all the pieces of the puzzle; she just had to fit them together. *I'm getting closer. I just can't quite...* she fell asleep mid-thought.

Chapter 26

Uproar at the Station
Lizzy Ruminates

At six the next morning, Jason and Harvey arrived at the station to find Barker asleep on the metal folding chair outside the holding cells.

"Barker?" The voice-activated recorder clicked on, and Barker's eyes snapped open. "Why don't you head home and get some sleep?"

"I'll wait until after the meeting."

"It's not for a couple more hours. You could at least have a lie-down in the break room."

"Honestly, I'm worried if I get too comfortable, I might be out for the duration. Why don't we listen to last night's recording? It's pretty interesting."

They moved into Jason's office and plugged the recorder into his computer. He was taking notes, Harvey at his feet and Barker snoring, when Chief Montgomery arrived at eight.

"We have a lot to discuss this morning." The chief sat in the guest chair. "Why is Barker sleeping?"

"He's been up all night. Where's everyone else?"

"They're coming."

Jason elbowed Barker, whose eyes opened slightly slower than the last time. "Let's swap chairs, Chief, so you can lead the meeting."

Chief Montgomery crossed his arms and leaned back. "I'm fine right here."

When all six officers had squeezed into the office, the chief said, "We have a lot to cover. Let's begin with Tate and Barker: the sabotaging kids."

Tate stood. "We discovered that three families, four kids, were involved."

"They're the same people who've been pushing for a homeowners' association in that neighborhood," Barker mumbled. "They don't like change."

"Anyway, I've compiled a list of their movements and their 'pranks,' as they call them, and I've updated the incident board. They didn't have any pertinent information to add."

"They did, actually." Barkers eyes opened a little wider. "They can verify the volunteers' statements. For example, they saw Holly downstairs after they changed the clue in the bathroom and headed for the secret passage. That was just after Mavis got into the jam."

Rodriguez approached Barker and leaned over his chair. "What does that have to do with anything? Are you still trying to cover up for her?"

Harvey growled deep in his throat.

"Who said I'm trying to cover for her? It was just an example."

"You guys asked for help, and every time we turn around, you're ignoring protocol," Rodriguez said. "You're a joke. The captain's precious little sister should be behind bars."

Barker stood and gave him a shove, then cocked his arm and punched him in the face.

Rodriguez took two steps backward. His eyes narrowed as he grabbed his bleeding nose. Then he attacked. Without much room to maneuver, everyone backed away—except the chief, who stayed seated, and Jason, holding Harvey's lead in a death grip.

"Harvey. Heel." Jason stood and seized Rodriguez's right fist mid-flight. "Barker, sit down, please. I can't afford to lose you. Rodriguez, that's enough."

"Sure. Protect him like you protect your sister," Rodriguez sneered.

"If you bait someone, you might expect a reaction. Yet you persist."

Rodriguez opened his mouth to speak, but the chief interrupted.

"I know you want to return to Sioux Falls, but if I send you back, you'll be placed on unpaid leave. Make your choice."

Rodriguez returned to his seat and glared at Barker.

Jason sat and gave Harvey a soothing pet. "Good boy," he murmured.

"Now," the chief continued as if nothing had occurred. "Please pass out your summary, Tate, and we'll move on to the interview with Lucian Basile and his attorney."

Rodriguez remained silent, so Deputy Nettle stood. "Mr. Basile was uncooperative, sir. The only thing he admitted to was searching for an urn containing his grandfather's ashes. He claims that Sage Fickle has the ashes and refuses to return them."

"We have some additional information, recorded last night when Serena Klein was brought in," Jason said.

"Is it admissible?" the chief asked.

"Yes. Barker warned them they weren't to speak and that if they did, they would be recorded."

Chief Montgomery nodded. "Proceed."

"Barker."

"When Ms. Klein was brought in, Lucian asked her why she was there, but she didn't answer. Then he asked her why she didn't just leave Prichard, and she admitted she wasn't Madeline. He asked her why she needed to pretend she was, and she told him Maddy always got everything she wanted. She wanted to trick Prichard so she could get the house he inherited. The conversation was a lot longer and more detailed, but that was the gist of it."

"We still need to interview her and find out what happened to Madeline," Jason said.

"Has any of this information gotten us closer to finding out who murdered Christine Luc?" the chief asked.

His question was met with silence.

Lizzy's day began much as any other. Holly had kindly taken Mavis outside and fed the animals, and then she started coffee and French toast. A slave to her stomach, Lizzy woke to the smell of breakfast and appeared in the kitchen before Holly could call her.

At Holly's feet, Mavis stared with sharp concentration.

"Good morning, Mavis," Lizzy called in jest, not expecting even the brief glance she got in response.

Mrs. Fickle snickered.

"How's her ESP working this morning? Breakfast smells delicious."

Holly giggled. "It's not quite up to snuff. I haven't dropped anything yet. Maybe she's waiting for bacon."

"Are we having bacon?"

"No."

"You're waiting in vain, puppy."

Holly carried a plate piled high with French toast to the table and sat down. "My mom invited us all over for dinner."

"Would it be alright if I pass today? I have some things I need to work on."

"Are you sure? She's making steak."

Lizzy nodded distractedly.

"Mom wants to see Candy. Should I take Mavis too?"

"No, I'd like her to stay with me."

Holly tilted her head like a little bird but didn't comment.

"I'll do the dishes," Lizzy said. "You two go ahead and get ready."

"Thanks. She's going to pick us up in twenty minutes."

"Thank you for breakfast. Have fun and say hi to your mom for me."

Deep in thought as she washed the dishes, she didn't hear them leave. After she finished, she sat on the sofa and stared at the fire, watching the flames curl around the dry wood, listening to the crackle and pop.

Marmalade stood in the middle of Mavis' bed and stretched mightily. Then she crossed the two feet separating Mavis' bed from her own and swatted her behind. *Whap, whap, whap* went her paw in rapid succession. Mavis got up quickly and left.

Lizzy wondered why Marmalade did that. Mavis wasn't bothering her; she wasn't doing anything. *Was she just being mean? Was she jealous?* Lizzy wasn't entirely sure about animal emotions.

Mavis hopped up on the sofa and laid her head on Lizzy's leg, looking up at her with mesmerizing brown eyes. "You'll protect me, won't you?" she seemed to say.

Lizzy stroked her ears. "Poor puppy." She looked at Marmalade again and thought, *What if it wasn't ever about Christine? What if it wasn't even about Holly? Who would suffer the most if something happened to her?*

Chapter 27

Fatal Mistake

Holly returned alone that evening, carrying a casserole. "Are you hungry?" she asked.

"Starving. I forgot to eat lunch."

"Did you get your work done?"

Lizzy nodded. It wasn't work, but she got it figured out.

Holly set the casserole dish on the kitchen table, and Mavis went crazy. She flew around the kitchen, through the living area, under Lizzy's desk, and back into the kitchen, where she took an acrobatic leap onto one of the chairs and another onto the table. Lowering her head, she bulldozed the casserole off the table with her snout. Globs of meat and noodles, interlaced with shards of ceramic, splattered across the tile floor like shrapnel. The startling sound of ceramic hitting tile was followed by Mavis' long howl as she stood stiff legged at the edge of the table, looking down at her destruction.

Lizzy, momentarily dumbstruck asked, "Holly? Where did you get that casserole?"

Holly's eyes widened. "Rice gave it to me with her condolences about the clinic. She was going to work for me, you know, but she only lasted a few hours."

"Was that before Mrs. Fickle was poisoned?"

Holly's mouth opened, but no sound emerged.

"Don't touch that. Call Jason. Tell him to call an ambulance so she thinks she succeeded. I'm going to take Mavis upstairs."

The dog struggled to get down when Lizzy picked her up. Her long body and four legs wiggled and squirmed, making it difficult to hold on.

Lizzy carried her upstairs to her bedroom.

"Thank you, Mavis. You're such a good guard dog. Your work is done for now. We won't eat it." She hugged her and kissed the top of her head. "I'll be back in just a little while."

She could hear Mavis barking behind the closed door but needed her out of the way when Jason arrived.

Pounding on the door signaled his arrival. "What happened?" he demanded when she opened the door. "Holly called me." His face was flushed, and Lizzy could see the rise and fall of his chest.

She put a hand on his arm. "We're okay. Mavis warned us. I think I know why Christine was killed and who did it. You need to have this casserole tested for poison, so we have proof." Lizzy indicated the congealing mass on the kitchen floor.

"Why did you ask for an ambulance?"

"We want her to think she succeeded so she doesn't run."

"Who?"

"Pearl Rice."

"Rice? You must be mistaken."

"It all fits."

After Lizzy explained her plan, Jason said, "Anyone else would say you've gone right off the deep end. How can you expect me to blindly do what you're asking?"

"If I'm wrong, what harm will it do to test the casserole? If I'm right, you've just solved five open cases."

"All based on a dog going nuts over a casserole."

"I wish you could have seen it."

"Okay. I'll do it. What happens if the test comes back positive?"

"Then we ask Dave if we can have a little after-hours surprise party for Rice." Lizzy winked.

———————— ··◄══►·· ————————

Jason directed the paramedics to load two stretchers into the ambulance and drive to the hospital without their siren, as they would for a deceased passenger.

He gave them a sample of the casserole with instructions for the lab, then called Steve to meet them there.

Wandering into the living area, he could hear Mavis' barking upstairs and murmured conversation coming from the kitchen. *I must be out of my mind. Why do I believe her crazy ideas?* He knew why. It was because, however she came to her final conclusions, she had always been right. This time he was going out on a limb.

He called Chief Montgomery to report. Unsure how to bring up Lizzy's strange belief in Mavis' poison-detecting abilities, he said, "I'll explain later, but we're having the casserole tested now and need to maintain a visual on former–Officer Rice."

"I trust your judgment. I'll assign Rodriguez and Tate to supper and surveillance at the diner and stand by."

"Thank you, sir."

Shortly thereafter, Steve called from the hospital. "I don't know how you knew, but the sample you sent to the lab contained enough potassium cyanide to kill an elephant. I hope no one ate any. Where'd it come from?"

"No one ate any, but let's just keep that to ourselves. You're invited to a party tonight at Dave's."

I shouldn't be surprised, Jason thought as he disconnected. *Let's see what she decides to do next.*

Lizzy was eating, of course. Holly had defrosted leftovers.

"Tag, you're it," he said. "Do you have enough for me?"

⸺⸱⸱⸺⟨ᴄ⟩⸺⸱⸱⸺

"It's a good thing we had those cooking lessons last month, or we'd probably starve." Lizzy savored her last bite of ham, salty and sweet with pineapple glaze. As she ate, she contemplated phase two of her plan. *First, I'll call Dave, then I'll write a posthumous letter for Jason to read. Should he read it beforehand or be surprised with the others?*

She picked up her phone and dialed.

"Hi, Dave. This is Lizzy. I wonder if you could do me a big favor."

"Sure. Whatever I can. What do you need?"

"We'd like to throw a surprise party for Pearl Rice tonight, and I was wondering if we could host it in the bar."

"A surprise party? What for? Is it her birthday?"

"Shh. I don't want her to know. Maybe you could have her help with the setup so she'll for sure be there?"

"You should really plan ahead a little more, but we don't have anything scheduled tonight. I can close early if you want to have it around ten."

"Thanks, Dave. Tables for around twenty people and a podium in front. Maybe some of your amazing sampler platters?"

"You've got it."

"Great. Remember, mum's the word." Lizzy hung up and smiled at Jason. "Phase one complete." She told him her plans for the letter.

"I think I'd like to read it ahead of time so I can focus on observing everyone's reactions. Is that okay?"

"Sure. I'll get to work."

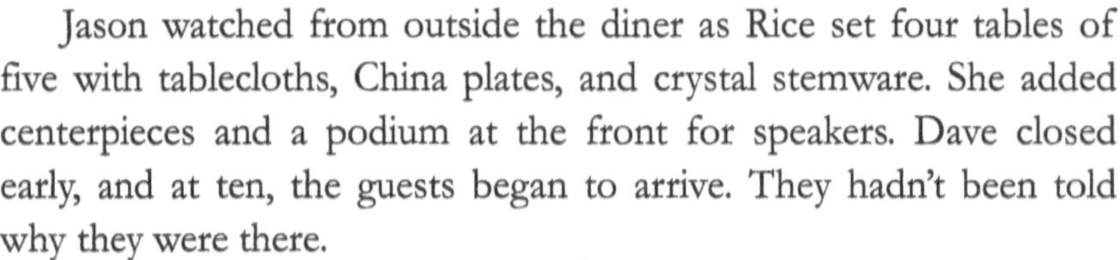

Jason watched from outside the diner as Rice set four tables of five with tablecloths, China plates, and crystal stemware. She added centerpieces and a podium at the front for speakers. Dave closed early, and at ten, the guests began to arrive. They hadn't been told why they were there.

Rodriguez and Tate remained alert and moved toward the exits as Rice greeted Dottie and Steve Peele. Chief Montgomery arrived with Sage Fickle. They were followed by Napoleon and Madeline Prichard. Nettle arrived with Serena Klein and sat her next to Madeline.

Moving closer to the window, Jason watched the sisters' first meeting in years.

Serena glanced at Madeline, then quickly looked away. Madeline recoiled from her, leaning toward her husband. Neither of them spoke.

Barker, the last to arrive, escorted Lucian Basile to Mrs. Fickle's table. Once everyone was seated, Jason strode into the diner, holding a sheaf of paper in his right hand.

He approached the podium and said, "Welcome to this evening's surprise party. Dave, Rice, please find seats at one of the tables."

"Who's the party for?" Napoleon asked.

"That's the surprise," Jason said. He cleared his throat and rustled the papers he was holding. "As you know, Lizzy was a writer, and she loved solving puzzles. After she and Holly were taken to the hospital this evening, I found this letter among her belongings, and I'd like to read it to you."

The room filled with whispered questions, as the guests shifted in their chairs and wondered aloud what happened to the two young women. Jason paid close attention to their postures and facial expressions, noting Steve put his hand on Dottie's. Dave's eyebrows rose, and Rice assumed a neutral expression.

Jason placed the papers on the podium and began to read:

> *As I observed Cleo strike Mavis for no apparent reason, it occurred to me that sometimes people's motivations aren't necessarily what they seem. I wondered if perhaps the deaths and misadventures that have recently plagued Harperstown might not have anything to do with the victims. Holly, a potential victim and carefully framed, might have only been an incidental target. Who, I thought, would suffer most if something were to happen to Holly?*

He listened to the whispering and studied the guests' demeanors, then continued:

> *I don't believe Christine Luc was ever the intended victim. She just couldn't pass up a drink.*

In fact, an eyewitness saw her and the murderer laughing about a joke they were going to play on Holly—we'll get back to that. Christine died and Holly wasn't arrested, despite an overabundance of evidence pointing at her. How frustrating for the murderer.

Jason stopped reading to find his audience leaning forward, waiting to hear more. He could have heard a pin drop. Rice seemed to be holding her breath.

So, the murderer tried again. Pastries from a trusted shop filled with a drug from Holly's clinic. It didn't matter if Holly died, or if she was convicted of murder. Either would do. But guess what? She didn't die, and she wasn't arrested. Instead, a completely innocent woman was sent to the hospital.

"That was me." Mrs. Fickle raised her hand.

Our murder became increasingly frustrated and flew into a rage when the eyewitness to her initial 'joke' came forward. She was approached by Serena Klein, posing as her sister, Madeline.

"You can see them here." Jason indicated the sisters, and the guests craned their necks to see. "They're identical." He waited a moment and continued.

Serena told the murderer she wanted money for her silence. I will assume she didn't mean for Madeline to die. What sister could do that to her own flesh and blood? But our murderer took her threat seriously and quickly hatched a plan. Madeline accepted the unexpected offer to coffee. On the way, she felt a prick in her arm and thought she had a bug bite, but that prick was a needle, and the result was a long slumber. She was left to die in the snow without a coat or shoes.

Everyone present was entranced. Rice looked at Serena and Madeline with a frown.

Once that little hiccup was taken care of, the murderer came up with another plan. Again, it didn't matter if Holly died, or if she was accused of murder.

Setting the animal hospital on fire and assuming Holly was sleeping in her house next door, the murderer figured she might burn in her bed or in the clinic, trying to rescue her patients. How did the murderer know about the phenobarbital and the recovering animals? She pretended to take a job at the clinic, then unexpectedly quit after several hours.

Dave gaped at Rice, who carefully avoided looking at him. *How did we finally discover the identity of our murderer, you ask? She tried to poison us with a hand-delivered casserole. It sure smelled good, Pearl Rice, but Mavis wouldn't let us eat it.*

Every person in that room stared at Rice, who looked like she was still trying to process what Jason had just read.

"What did you just say?" she asked.

"Would you like me to read it again? Or perhaps you'd like Lizzy to explain it in person."

Lizzy and Holly entered the room. Rice got up and ran. Not toward the exit, but in Holly's direction. Hands extended, she reached for Holly's neck, shrieking in anger and frustration. She was detained by Sergeant Rodriguez before she could make contact.

Jason approached her and asked, "Why didn't you just come after me?"

"That would have been too easy on you. You ruined my life. You locked up the man I love and took away my career, my self-respect, my standing in the community, my future. I want you to suffer."

"Didn't it occur to you that you did all those things to yourself?" Jason asked gently. "I haven't hired anyone else because I kept wishing you could come back."

Rice yelled and fought against Rodriguez' hold. "I hate you so much," she spat. "I would kill you with my bare hands if I could."

Jason could still hear her screaming after Rodriguez and Tate led her outside to the waiting cruiser.

Chapter 28

How Did You Know?

During the stunned silence as the cruiser pulled away, Dave made a half-hearted wave at Bob, waiting behind the bar. Bob brought platters of finger foods to the tables.

Serena looked at Lizzy and asked, "How did you know?"

"It was two things really. I remembered seeing the light on the dumbwaiter in the basement on Saturday afternoon, but the hatch was closed. It was noisy when it moved. When we went upstairs, Rice, who wasn't scheduled to be there, was loitering around the door to the basement. She said she arrived at a time when the doors were locked, and she didn't know about the meeting. And then there was your perfume. I smelled it in the basement, and also in the secret room upstairs. I think you were hiding in the dumbwaiter, and she heard it move. She wanted to know who was in it and what they saw."

Serena said, "I'm so sorry, Maddy. I never meant for her to kill you. I swear I didn't."

Madeline looked away.

Then to Lizzy, Serena said, "She and Christine were laughing about playing a joke on Holly Schneider. I saw Rice put something in a bottle. Then she told Christine to offer it to Holly to get her into trouble with Dottie. She warned her not to drink it herself."

"Why were you in the dumbwaiter?"

"Lucian told me to hide until you closed for the day. I was helping him find his grandfather's ashes."

"Is that what you've been looking for?" Mrs. Fickle asked Lucian.

"You knew that."

"No, I didn't. You never told me."

"Can I have them?"

"You can, but those old stories about an urn filled with treasure are just stories. It's only special if you want to keep grandfather by your side."

"I'll tell you about that later."

Mrs. Fickle nodded.

"Did you ever figure out how Holly's prints got on the glass?" Jason asked.

"During our dress rehearsal, Dr. Steve and I walked in on Rice ostensibly jumping in front of Holly to protect her from Christine. I think she and Christine were putting on a little show, and before Rice took up her stance, she shoved the glass she was holding into Holly's hands."

"What about her own prints?"

"She was still wearing gloves, which I thought was strange at the time, but I forgot about it. Holly put the glass on the sewing table before she went downstairs and also forgot about it until I brought it up this evening."

"That's why her prints were at a strange angle," Barker said. "I wondered about that. What about the decanter?"

"The doc was right about that. Holly remembered picking it up from the floor when she got her sock wet," Jason said. "How did you figure out what happened to Madeline?"

"Once I realized Rice was responsible, everything fell into place. She didn't know about Serena; she thought it was Madeline who tried to blackmail her. Serena would have been more cautious getting into the car with her, but her sister was completely unaware of the potential danger."

"I almost died. Why would you do that?" Madeline asked. "I know we don't get along, but... Why?"

Serena looked down and picked at her fingernails. "I've been so stupid and selfish. I didn't realize how dangerous she was.

"I just wanted you out of the way so Napoleon would think I was you and give me the house."

"This was all because of the stupid house? The one with the giant hole in the roof? You almost got me killed for a worthless house?"

"I'm sorry," Serena whispered. "I told you I was stupid."

Mr. Prichard put his hand on Madeline's. "I'm sorry about the house, honey. I've asked a professional to help with the tree, and I'll fix it. You can even remodel it how you want."

"You asked someone for help?"

"Yer. Just for you."

Jason wandered over to Dave and placed his hands on his shoulders. "Don't take it so hard old man."

"I thought I'd found the woman of my dreams."

"She fooled us all."

"Bob," Dave called, "open bar. I think we could all use a drink. Me first." He stood and moved to the bar.

Jason saw the chief stride toward Lizzy, so he headed in that direction. *Damage control,* he thought.

"Very nice work, Ms. Hornwhistle," the chief said. "You've just solved all our open cases."

Lizzy opened her mouth to respond, then closed it when Jason whispered, "Don't tell him about Mavis."

"Jason and I make a pretty good team," she said.

"Indeed, you do. Perhaps we should give you a job."

"Thank you, Chief, but I already have a job," she said with a smile.

Chapter 29

Supper with the Schneiders

The view from Lizzy's front window was unbearable. All Holly's dreams, everything she had worked so hard for, had gone up in smoke. She knew Lizzy wanted to help, but she didn't know how to express her grief. Her irrepressible optimism had for once deserted her. As she turned and retreated to the sofa, Candy meowed and looked up with her sweet little face.

"You understand, don't you, precious? What should I do now?" Holly stroked her soft fur.

"Maybe we should take a road trip," Lizzy said from behind her.

"How would that help? I just got back from my vacation."

"I set up a GoFundMe account for you, and combined with the insurance money, you have plenty to rebuild. The contractors can begin as soon as the site is released. You and I can rent an RV and take Mavis and Candy on an adventure while they build your new clinic. What do you say?"

Not quite ready to give up her bout of maudlin self-pity, she couldn't help but feel a spark of interest. "Where would we go?"

"I guess that depends on how much adventure you want." Lizzy's eyes danced. "I've been invited to speak at a conference in Los Angeles."

"Doesn't that scare you?"

"Yes. But if you're with me, it won't be quite as scary. And think about it. We can trade our parkas for swimsuits."

"But… You worked so hard to disappear."

"That's the adventure part. I have a wig. We can come up with a plan. Kirk said he'll help us."

Lizzy's enthusiasm was contagious.

As her excitement rose, Holly's heart thumped in her chest. "What about your writing?"

"I might have to write a little during our trip because sometimes I can't ignore it. But I'll try my best to just enjoy myself."

"Have you started something new?"

"I have an idea, but it might have to wait. I thought I might have Rachel investigate a church-related conspiracy. I asked Penelope Turnbull how I could learn more about the church."

"Isn't she amazing? When I talk to her, I feel like… I don't know. It seems like I can feel God's presence. Does that sound weird?"

"I don't really know what that means, but she does have a strong, comforting demeanor."

"My mom invited us for supper tonight, and she invited the Turnbulls too. You can get to know them.

"We can tell them about our trip too. You'll come, right?

"I wouldn't miss it." Holly grinned.

Lizzy loved visiting the Schneider home. Holly's parents, like their home, were warm and inviting. As soon as they arrived, Lizzy ran into the kitchen and hugged Thelma Schneider. Like her son, she was tall and lean with curly red hair and green eyes. Holly took more after her father who, although not short, was stocky with brown hair. His stern bearing reflected his long military career, but his obvious love for his family shone through.

Thelma laughed and held her arms up. "Let me wipe my hands before you're covered with flour. I'm so glad to see you." She washed her hands and gave Lizzy a big hug. "I hear you've been out solving crime again."

"Not really. I think it was Mavis."

"She's a pretty smart cookie. Did you bring her along?"

"Absolutely. She would never forgive me if I left her at home. What're we having? It smells delicious."

"I made chicken parmesan, especially for you."

"Yum, yum, yum." Lizzy hopped up and down as her stomach growled loudly, and Thelma laughed.

"Where's Mrs. Fickle?"

"I think she's taking a little nap. Would you like a glass of wine while you wait?"

"I don't want to ruin my appetite."

"No chance of that," Jason said as he entered the kitchen. He handed Lizzy and his mother each a single red rose. "Happy Valentine's Day."

Lizzy sniffed the flower and smiled.

"Thank you, dear. Did you bring Barker with you?" his mother asked.

"It seems he's dating Holly now, so I can't get rid of him." He grinned and gave his mom a half hug.

"Take Lizzy into the den and give her a snack. We're still waiting for the Turnbulls."

"You heard the boss. Come with me."

"Thank you for the rose," she whispered.

Holly and Barker were sitting together on a loveseat and snacking from a tray of sliced summer sausage, cheese, and crackers.

"Oh, that's where you are," Lizzy said to Mavis.

"Yep. She's doing her best ESP. Steve's already dropped two pieces of meat."

Mr. Schneider had one eye on the television and the other on Holly. "Lizzy," he roared when she entered the room. "It's great to see you. Do you watch basketball?"

"I used to follow the Suns a bit," she said, sparking an enthusiastic conversation about Devin Booker that lasted until the Turnbulls arrived.

Thelma called them all into dinner, and Mr. Schneider reluctantly turned off the basketball game.

Once they were all seated around the dining room table, they joined hands, and Pastor Turnbull said a prayer of thanksgiving. "Heavenly Father, I thank you for our family and friends seated here together. Thank you for your Holy Spirit who is with us always, guiding us and giving us strength. Thank you for your infinite wisdom and grace. In Jesus' name we pray, Amen."

"Amen," everyone repeated.

Holly and her mother rose to carry plates of chicken parmesan and bowls of side dishes to the table. When they were seated again, the pastor took a bite and declared it delicious.

Lizzy almost swooned when she tried hers. The tender chicken, the delicate sauce, the melty cheese. She started at Jason's chuckle. "What?"

"You groaned over that bite. I was worried you might pass out."

"Be nice, Jason," his mother scolded.

"I'm just teasing. We all know how much Lizzy loves her food."

"Rooherer." Mavis, not to be outdone, made her presence known.

"Poor puppy," Mrs. Fickle said.

Lizzy snorted.

Mavis whined pitifully, ending in her strange new cooing sound.

"Did you miss supper?" Mrs. Schneider asked.

"She did not. Little scammer," Lizzy said.

"Is it okay if I give her a plate?"

"Yes, I suppose. Not too much though. She already looks like a football."

The pastor turned to Jason and said, "I'd like to hear how you fared after we met."

Jason smiled at him and said, "I suppose I owe you that."

That got everyone's attention. Jason looked around the table and said, "At one point during the investigation, I felt completely overwhelmed. So much was happening that we couldn't keep up. I didn't have time to sleep, let alone think, and I was afraid if I called Sioux Falls for help, they would arrest Holly.

"So, I went to talk to Pastor Turnbull."

"That's why Lizzy and I—"

Barker nudged Holly with his elbow and shook his head.

The pastor nodded. "Go ahead."

"I felt my stress and fear subside after he prayed with me, and then I realized he was right. I don't always have to do everything by myself. I called my chief and asked for help."

"Such a nice man," Mrs. Fickle said.

"Together, the six of us were able to investigate and, with Lizzy's help, we solved all five cases."

"It was Mavis," Lizzy said.

"God must have been looking out for us. Rice tried so hard to kill me. She didn't care who got hurt in the process."

"You may be right." Penelope put her hand over Holly's. "Lizzy expressed an interest in learning more about the church and our beliefs, and I suggested she talk to Marshall. But each of you can share with her as well. Personal experiences are often more illuminating than dogma."

"I… um…"

"I know dear. You were thinking of your book. But God works in mysterious ways to make himself known."

Lizzy looked down and took a bite of her chicken, willing herself to disappear. She was embarrassed and completely out of her element as the conversation continued around her. Mavis whined and stared at her, begging for another piece of chicken. "Incorrigible," she murmured, handing her a small piece.

As the guests finished their final bites, groaning and patting their stomachs, Thelma stood and said, "I hope you left room for dessert."

"I might pop," Lizzy said.

"It's homemade tiramisu."

"If we're taking bets, mine is on Lizzy making room," Jason said.

"Ditto," Holly said.

"You know me so well. Let me help serve. I need to get up and move around."

She and Holly served the tiramisu, and after they resumed their seats, Holly said, "We have some news."

All eyes were on her as she continued. "Lizzy and I are going to take a road trip while my clinic is being rebuilt."

"A road trip? Where?" Her mother asked.

"You tell them, Lizzy."

"We're going to rent an RV and drive to Los Angeles. I've been invited to speak at a writers' convention."

"Aren't you worried about the paparazzi?" Jason asked at the same time Barker asked, "Why don't you just fly?"

"I'll worry about you camping alone," Thelma said.

"How fun. Congratulations," Mrs. Fickle said.

Lizzy, unused to anyone caring about what she did, was bewildered. She canted her head.

"I've been moping around," Holly said, "and I think Lizzy's trying to cheer me up."

"It's a win-win. We'll have something new and exciting to try, and I'll have moral support. I can't do this alone."

"You'll never have to," Holly assured her with a smile.

Chapter 30

Last Night in Harperstown

Lizzy sat in her lavender recliner with Mavis, staring at the fire. She had only been living in Harperstown for two months, but it felt like a lifetime. She *did* want to go somewhere warm and sunny, but she wasn't ready to leave her new home. *I feel safe here. Comfortable.*

She thought about the irony. The past two weeks had been fraught with danger, but she felt safe. *It's because I'm not alone anymore. I have people.*

"And you, Mavis." She stroked her little dog's ears. "Never has there been a more gallant guard dog. You're such a clever girl."

Mavis wiggled, enjoying the attention.

"How much do you really understand?" Lizzy asked her.

Mavis was a slave to her stomach, just like Lizzy, but she seemed to know when something was unsafe to eat. Was that because Dennis had poisoned her before Christmas? She used to always bark at the bad guys, but she didn't bark at Rice. Was that because Rice used to work with Jason? Or because she dropped dog treats from her pockets? Or maybe because she didn't have bad intentions directed at Lizzy?

She shook her head. "I guess I'll never know but thank you for saving me. Twice. And thank you for helping me solve the case."

"Aroherer."

"It's not time yet."

Mavis hopped down from the recliner and barked twice, running toward the front door.

"Potty time?" Lizzy got up, and there was a knock on the door.

When she opened it, Jason and Harvey were standing on the porch. "May we come in?"

"Of course. I thought Mavis had to go outside, but I guess she was just telling me you were here."

Harvey lunged past her and chased Mavis around the sparse furniture populating the first floor.

"We're going to miss you," Jason said. He removed his coat and boots and followed Lizzy into the kitchen.

"I'll miss you too. I was just thinking that I'm not ready to leave town, even for a short time. I like it here. Want some coffee?"

"Yes, thanks. I wish I could go with you."

She could feel his eyes following her movements and struggled to remain lighthearted. "I wish I could take the whole town, but that wouldn't be very low profile, would it?"

He chuckled. "I guess not."

Mavis sat under his chair, anticipating crumbs, and Harvey lay on his belly, scooting closer.

Handing Jason a cup of coffee, Lizzy eyed Mavis and sat across the table. Her breath hitched when she looked into his eyes, something she consciously avoided most of the time, and noted a hint of vulnerability there. She swayed on the precipice, her traitorous tongue longing to say words she would never be able to take back, when Holly's entrance saved her from herself.

Dressed in her favorite red dress and the heels she had worn for the mystery maze, Holly said, "Steve and I are going out for a going-away supper date. Do I look okay?"

"You look gorgeous," Lizzy said. "Is he okay with our trip?"

Holly smiled. "He's always very sensible. Right now, he's trying to figure out how he can use some leave and meet up with us in LA."

"Darn. I guess that means I can't," said Jason. "Someone has to man the fort."

"Want to order pizza, since you just got here?"

"Pizza and dogs. Sounds great."

"We could watch a movie."

"Or play cards."

Lizzy scrunched up her nose. "That still reminds me of Theo. It might be a while before I want to play again."

"We'll think of something."

"Right." When the doorbell rang, Lizzy said, "Don't be too late. We're leaving early."

"What's a little sleep deprivation between friends?" Holly said with a wink.

Be the lovely who
Kindly leaves a review

Thank you so much for reading.

Booksellers may purchase multiple copies of this
book at a discount from IngramSpark.

Mother of two, cat mom, and prolific reader, Alice Kanaka is the author of nine mystery novels, numerous short stories, and a twelve-episode collaboration with Black Knight, author of the *Starshatter* space opera series.

Alice holds a bachelor's degree in Spanish and a Master of Business Administration with a concentration in Human Resources. She spent twelve years working at a state psychiatric hospital, speaks three languages, and has lived in seven countries.

A life-long fan of the mystery genre, Alice's books combine traditional tropes with contemporary characters to create whodunits that are simultaneously familiar and unique. Her aspiration is to write books that she would enjoy reading; stories that are both entertaining and uplifting, perfect with a cup of Earl Grey and a roaring fire on a gloomy day.

HTTPS://AliceKanaka.com